LET THEM IN

BY: LISAH JAYNE WALDEN

LET THEM IN

CONTENTS

THE FIFTH FLOOR

I had to get these papers written. This was my last chance to turn my life around. My fellow cocktail waitresses at Dynasty Lounge thought I had been nuts to trade in my high heels for books, but my children were getting older. The last thing I needed was for my sons to realize that their mommy worked at a titty bar. I scurried to the campus library checkout desk, only to find that of course, all of the study rooms were unavailable. I grabbed my suitcase full of notebooks and textbooks off the floor and stomped off to the elevator. If this wasn't a metaphor for my life nothing was. Number three. Press. Sigh. Lean. The doors of the elevator opened, and I raced around the third floor trying to find a couch, a cubicle, a seat, maybe just a damn corner. Nothing! Everything was already occupied. What really pissed me off were all the people lying asleep on the couches.

"Are you serious?" I breathed loudly, hoping I could wake them up. God, go to your damn room if you want to sleep.

I huffed to the elevator. Number four, again press. Again sigh. Yet again lean. Fourth floor, same bullshit, same occupied spaces. I re-entered the elevator and slung my suitcase against the wall. The elevator didn't move. Forgot to press a number. I swung around and glared at the buttons, but there was nowhere else to go. This was the last floor. That's when I saw the glowing number. Number five? But there wasn't a fifth floor. Sure, why not. Number five—press. Sigh.

The elevator dinged. The compartment dropped a quarter of an inch before the doors slid open. I crept from the elevator and stood in a wide hallway. It seemed quiet enough. Good place to study. I began walking down the hallway then made a left turn. There were people studying in several of the cubicles. A girl peered over a laptop so intently that her glasses had begun to slide down the bridge of her nose. "Oh, thank God," I breathed. The girl with glasses threw me a stern glare. Her hair was a messy attempt at pigtails. An over-sized flannel shirt hung over her pale, thin frame.

In the distance, I heard heavy breathing. An *ugh, ugh, ugh* noise echoed down the hallway. I turned toward it and saw... a man doing backflips? I staggered sideways, knocking my suitcase to the floor. I did a double take. This is a library, right? The man stopped in front of me. Neither sheen nor shine gave away his exertions; it was only his tall, lean body that flexed from the rigorous workout. He lifted his index finger to his pink lips that turned up seductively in the corners. "Shh." He lowered his eyes to my breasts, his hand extended as if to touch them. I tried to retreat but was met with the cold, concrete wall of the library. He smiled at my discomfort, and continued his backflips down the hall.

I stood there for a moment, disoriented. Then, I noticed the students who had been studying. With the exception of the girl with glasses, who fervently typed away at her laptop, they were all looking up, their jaws dropped. They sat stiff, their mortal flesh turned to marble death, as if a gorgon had been here. I looked in the direction of their silent gaze. A giant, hairy wolf spider was dragging the struggling body of a teenage boy across the paisley wallpapered ceiling. The boy would have been screaming had it not been for all the webbing encased over his face. That's it. Had *enough*.

I was too scared to scream. Only hurried breath and a small whimper escaped my throat. I turned to run back to the elevator, my suitcase of books in tow, but halfway down the hall, I was met by a young girl dressed as a princess. She was surrounded by lily pads placed strategically on a blue carpet like a game of Twister. This hadn't been here before. A frog, adorned with a golden crown, hopped next to her. It stuck out its tongue. The girl bent over and swallowed the frog's tongue with her mouth. My throat closed up. My stomach hurled against my bowels. The girl stopped kissing the frog. It hopped in front of her. The girl, dressed in frills of silk and a purple and pink chemise, screamed and drew a butcher knife from behind her. She held down the struggling frog and lopped off its legs. She placed a leg in her mouth and dragged the frog's meat apart from the bone with her teeth. The princess then licked the blood off her fingers, peered up at me, and smiled.

"The French could never keep their promises." She offered me the other leg.

My stomach heaved as bile and coffee filled my mouth. I forced myself to swallow it. Jesus, my kids. I didn't have a will, or life insurance, or a plan. Run. I had to run. I was back where the spider had carried the boy, and where a man had performed backflips to enforce library courtesy.

Where was my suitcase? I must have left it in the hallway with the princess. I looked behind me and saw her sucking the brains out of the frog prince's head. She twirled the tiny crown around her index finger. She sucked and sucked until all that was left was its skin and tiny fragile bones. The princess dropped the carcass to the floor and picked up her shiny golden ball. She stood up and placed her right foot on my suitcase. Her little lips were pursed; pale-blonde eyebrows lifted and laughed. She threw the ball high in the air and caught it, all the while never taking her murky blue eyes off me. She repeated this juggling act with the agility of a carny.

"Don't you want to play with me?" she asked.

I looked at the frog carcass. "No."

She screamed and threw her golden ball at me. I fell to the floor as the globe exploded like a cannonball in the wall behind me. Her toy came back through the wall, a spherical boomerang, returning to the palm of the princess. "Play with me!"

I must be dreaming. I must have fallen asleep, exhausted from finals, and reading, and worry, and lack of food, and lack of fun. Maybe I broke down and started drinking. This was a drunkenmare.

Not real. Just a stupid dream, but dreams offer doors no matter how smashed the dreamer is, was, is? Shit. There had to be another way out of here. *Think, think, fucking think.* The other floors had stairs. Where were the stairs? I ran back to the cubicles where the students were still transfixed like gargoyles, gazing at the ceiling. The spider was gone. Probably enjoying its feast. They were still staring, though, all except for the girl in glasses. I ran towards her. Just as I was about to reach her, my feet became transfixed to the floor. My leg muscles stiffened, and my arms fell like a rigid corpse at my sides. Silver liquid crept like mercury up my legs, hardening as it moved along, becoming a strange rubber molding itself over every inch of my body.

"Stop struggling," the girl with glasses said. Her fingers pounded swiftly on a keyboard. The faster she typed, the faster the mercury liquid moved.

"You're doing this!" I glared at her—now unable to move my head, blink my eyes, or scratch the itch that tickled my nose.

"Shut up. I'm almost done," she replied. "Done."

There was a tingling sensation in my toes that slowly spread up my legs to my ribcage. Everywhere this suit had covered was now tingling. My feet loosened up, and I almost fell forward. Whatever was holding me had ceased its grasp.

"Pick up that knife," she said.

"What knife?"

"The knife on the table," she said.

There was nothing on the table. "There's no knife," I replied.

"What?" She looked past her laptop. "Damn." Her fingers pounded the keyboard. A dagger appeared right in front of me on the table. "There. Now pick it up and cut me loose."

"How is that possible? How is all of this possible?"

"I don't have time for this. Cut me loose."

I picked up the blade and walked towards her, where I could now see that a gigantic vine had wrapped itself around the girl's legs, binding her to the chair. It wrapped itself so tightly around her calves and thighs that blood had started to seep through her jeans. Every now and then she winced from the pain. The vine was spreading its trap, slowly sprouting towards her ribcage.

"What the hell are you looking at? Cut me loose," she said as beads of sweat pooled on her forehead.

"Not until you tell me what's going on," I said.

"I had to write you in order to get out of here. Now, cut—"

"Wait. What?"

"You. I wrote you. You're just a character. Now do as I say and cut me loose."

"That's not right. I have children. I have a life." My head was swimming.

"That's just exposition. Blah, blah, blah. I created you. Now do as I say."

I wanted to bury the knife into her skull. Or did she write me to want that? No. My life was real. It had meaning. My boys, my struggles, and the disgusting men I dealt with to keep my sons in diapers and fed with baby formula. The way I struggled to feed them while trying to get my degree. Character? Her creation? If it was true, then she was the cruelest bitch I had ever seen. Character? I'll show her character.

"Don't even think about it. If I die here, so will you." She had her finger over the delete button. I rushed her, the knife less than an inch from her temple. "You kill me," she whispered, "then you'll definitely have no place else to go. Do you wanna get out of here or what?" She turned toward me slowly, still wincing from the vine's embrace. Her lips were chapped and trembling, her fingers calloused, almost bloody.

"What about them?" I motioned at the frozen students, my knife still at her temple.

"Failed attempts who wouldn't listen. The fifth floor took them over." She looked down the hall, anticipating a new monster. What would be next? Stephen King's It? My nagging mother? With the way this place was, I wouldn't doubt it. "You need me as much as I need you, so cut—me—loose."

"Play with ME!" That voice. *The princess.* My bowels ached. Shit. I forgot about the princess.

"Oh my god! Cut me loose! Cut me loose!" She thrashed against the vine pinning her to the chair, causing more blood to seep from her wounds to her jeans. The princess tilted her head up and sniffed the air. She licked her lips then looked back at us. She turned her focus to the girl in glasses. She breathed in the air and licked her lips again.

I knelt down and began to hack and saw through the base of

the large vine that intruded from the carpet. As much as I hated laptop girl right now, I saw how the princess smelled her blood. I remembered the frog prince. At the final stroke of the knife, her chair fell over. The greenery snapped. The vine came to life and thrashed against the floor. It whipped against my leg, attempting to grab hold of me. It took hold of my leg, and then a strange sound spilled from the vine, almost like a child screaming. I looked and saw the vine sizzle as if the mercury-like suit had burned it.

"Why won't you play with me?" The princess's voice played the singsong, disturbing lullaby of a homicidal brat. I could hear the *boing, boing, boing* of her golden ball bouncing. Curious. How could a ball bounce that previously acted as a weapon? I guess in this world, just about anything could happen. World? Did I even have a world? Was I *really* just a made-up character? Anger burned. My suit started to glow. The girl in glasses moved away from me.

"There you are. Oh! How pretty. You're shiny." The princess skipped towards us.

"Get the laptop," the girl in glasses whispered.

"Just like my ball." The princess's voice had dropped two octaves into a masculine growl. She opened her mouth wider than seemed possible. Rows of sharp, shark-like teeth jutted from her jaw. I grabbed the laptop and tossed it to the girl with glasses. Immediately her fingers pounded the keyboard. The princess laughed. She cast the ball at me again. The globe caught me square in the gut and flung me against the wall behind me, which splintered from the impact. Aside from having the wind knocked out of me, I was actually fine. I stepped away from it as the plaster fell to the carpet. I grabbed the damn ball in the palm of my hand before it could leave my gut to return to its owner. The golden globe vibrated against my palms. Every emotion, every bit of rage and terror—mainly rage—flowed from me into her little ball.

The princess thrust out her hand, reaching for her golden ball. As she tried to pull it from me, I felt it try to leave, but I held it tightly. She stomped her foot. She pulled her hand back then thrust it forward again. The ball shifted in my grasp. As I continued to fuel it with my anger, it tingled slightly, then vibrated and hummed, glowing in my palm.

"Give me back my ball," the princess said.

"You want me to play with you, little bitch?" The ball vibrated harder in my palm. My arm wrenched back. My shoulder extended with such force that my fingertips shook. Her golden globe carried my message back to her. Blind curls gleamed under the fluorescent ceiling lights as her head rolled down the hallway. Eventually, her golden globe returned back to me.

"Wow, I didn't expect that to happen," the girl in glasses said, her fingers still at the keyboard, not typing, just still.

"I thought you were the writer."

"Yeah, so did I. Guess you have more a mind of your own than I thought."

"It would appear so," I returned. I had some ideas of what was going on, but I didn't want to let her in on it. I decided to see how it all panned out.

"Come on," she said getting up. "There's a stairwell over here."

I followed her. Her shell-shocked body hugged the wall. I walked in the open. I didn't need cover anymore. I had this great suit and this badass golden ball. We found the staircase. She pushed the door open and ran without looking. The staircase ended on the third step with nothing but a clear drop. She fell but managed to hold onto the third step. She tried to hoist herself up. I could see her face appear over the stairs as she lifted herself onto the third stair. Her leg was bleeding terribly. The laptop was on the cement floor next to my foot. I picked it up and placed it next to her hand. It was dark down there, past that drop. Couldn't see a thing. But it wasn't empty. There were all sorts of noises, whisperings, and growls.

"Help me up," she grunted.

I kneeled next to her. "Funny, how you didn't see that coming."

"What the—Just help me up!" She winced and pressed her hand to her bleeding leg.

"No, I don't think so. Seems you have everything you need right there at your fingertips. Why don't you write yourself out of this jam?"

"If I die, you die."

"I don't think so. You typed me, made me—so you say. Well, what brought you here? I have the smokin' costume, and this fabulous little ball. I destroyed that bitch of a princess. If anything, I'm the main character, and you—you're just the sidekick." Her eyes widened as her jaw dropped. I had struck a nerve. "You really should get typing. Something down there sounds hungry."

I threw the ball in the air, caught it in my palm. Turned on my heel and left her in the stairwell. I walked around the corner towards the elevator, was about to push the down button, but thought maybe I should stay for a bit. See what else I could find on the fifth floor.

THE AWAKENING

The car lulled her, but Elizabeth had given up on sleep. She couldn't even be angry anymore. She couldn't remember the last time that she really slept—that deep sleep where the mind is at ease, and there are no dreams remembered. It had been years since she felt like that. Or was it decades? Maybe once when she was a child she slept like that, but not now. Now was filled with the hunt. Now Drew was at the wheel, and Elizabeth hated relinquishing control. She scooched up in her seat.

"How far are we?" Elizabeth said, grabbing her sunglasses from the dash and placing them over her bloodshot eyes.

"About ten miles." Drew lit a cigarette.

"Did I sleep that long?" Elizabeth rolled down her window and watched the world pass.

"Nope. I just drive that fast."

"Well, keep it legal, speed racer. We don't need the attention."

She fumbled for her water bottle and realized it was empty. Drew handed her a full bottle. "Thanks," she said. She looked at him and shook her head. He still wore that ridiculous red and brown striped hat half-lifted off the top of his head. What's the sense of wearing a hat if it's not firmly on your head?

"You sure love that water," he said.

"I need it." Elizabeth gulped half of it down and set it in the cup holder. She opened the glove compartment and retrieved the desiccated succubus scalp. Nothing had changed. Their next kill would be in Rochester.

"You know what we could use?" She grinned at Drew. "Some fun."

"Oh, no. We don't need the attention, remember? The last time we, I mean *you*, had a little 'fun,' you knocked a guy out and had me digging through his pockets. No, we stick to our orders." Drew fished out one last handful of BBQ chips, crumpled up the bag, and threw it out the window.

"You know, we do have a garbage bag here."

Drew laughed. "I can't believe you care. Tell you what, you just lie back and get some Z's. I'll wake you once we get to Rochester."

Elizabeth turned on her side and stared out the window. The moon played on her luminescent pale skin. "Hoodlum," she said.

* * *

Annette was tired. Tired of the Pilates classes to trim her stomach and thighs, tired of shopping for home décor. She was tired of cooking beef Wellington and chicken french for Steven's friends, tired of coaxing her sixteen-year-old daughter to wear a shirt that didn't reveal so much cleavage. She counted down the hours until she could hide in her room, just her and the latest Julie James novel—wearing her flannel jammies and sipping her chai tea where she would disappear into a world unlike the complacent, suburban life she felt punished to live. No daughter to defy her. No husband to appease with the routine of a dinner that takes all day to make, how was your day, and the nightly courtship of oral sex and doggy style. God forbid he should actually look at her anymore when they had sex. Yes, Annette was tired—watching re-runs of *Friends* at two a.m. tired.

As usual, Annette had her cell phone on hand just in case the school called. She had hoped that Priya would have outgrown the bullying, mean spirit she had displayed in elementary school, but as her daughter grew older, Priya's actions only seemed to become more malicious.

Annette needed to get outside. She headed to the backyard in a pair of paint-stained yoga pants and an old Victoria's Secret t-shirt that read "Hair in a Bun and Getting Things Done." That about summed up her life. Her yard was the one thing Annette was truly proud of. It was perfectly manicured, down to the edges leading to the walkway and driveway.

She had even put together the pergola herself. Wisteria grew up the sides and covered the top of the structure. She had researched it for weeks, making sure that she picked a pergola that could support the weight of the vines. It took a good two years to get the wisteria established. There was the pinching and pruning, the shifting of the vines. Looking at those beautiful purple blossoms, Annette felt it was truly worth the sweat and the swearing and the frustration. Annette wiped the silly smile off her face and turned her attention to her vegetable garden.

Although Steven kept offering, nudging her to hire help, Annette refused to hire a gardener just as she refused to hire a housekeeper.

"What would be left for me to do then?" she responded once.

"You could go back into your photography, maybe join a book club, get out of the house and socialize."

"I don't want strangers in our home."

"You need to get out of the house. You to see your friends again."

"And talk about what? Their children and the lack of ours?!" She hadn't meant to shout at him. It wasn't his fault. It was the fault of her degraded eggs. She wanted children, Steve wanted children, but her womb wouldn't allow his sperm to seed. Soon after that argument, Steve and Annette agreed to try artificial insemination. They would have to use a donor egg. *Donor*. Annette laughed at how much they'd had to pay for that "donation."

She began with the sweet peas in raised beds in her vegetable garden. They were so delicate and frail. She used to call Priya her little sweet pea. She had been born two months premature, and Annette refused to leave her side. Every moment Annette was awake, she would be there with her daughter, touching her through the glass with gloved hands, attempting to keep the bond her womb had once again refused.

Annette gently pulled the weeds, her fingers deftly moving between the winding vines of the sweet peas, careful to not uproot her vegetables. The weeds had become so plentiful with all the summer rain, but soon she had finished with the sweet peas. She loved the taste of them. There was nothing like fresh, home-grown vegetables. Annette had moved on to her tomatoes when her cell phone rang, followed by a vibration. Over and over. Her hands were covered in mud. Annette knew she should have worn gardening gloves, but today she wanted to feel the soil, the vegetation, to carefully place the worms that had been uprooted by her weeding back into her gardens. She wiped her hands on the lawn, attempting to rid the soil from her fingers as much as she could before she stood up and retrieved her phone. She recognized the number. Priya's school.

"Hello." It was a statement, not a question. She knew who it was and why they were calling.

"Hello, Mrs. Robertson." Ms. Gonzalez again. She must have Annette's phone on speed dial.

"What did she do?" Annette sat on the grass and caressed the leaves of her tomato plant.

"Could you come down to the school?"

"I'm in the middle of something," Annette said.

"Well, I'm afraid your daughter has overstepped some bounds

here. She put a tack on a boy's chair, after she wrote the word 'PIG' across his locker."

Annette was usually well-equipped for these conversations, but this call was different from the rest: *boy, his.* Priya was a bully, true, but never to the boys. "I'm sorry, you said it was a *boy's* chair?"

"Yes, apparently she has been relentless with this young man for—"

"I'm sorry to interrupt again, but you said that Priya attacked a boy? That's so unlike her."

"I agree. Usually I have to call you about the young ladies your daughter, has, well, in your words, *attacked.* But, this incident with a certain young man escalated. It wasn't just the tack. He's in the nurse's office."

"Is he okay?" Annette walked to her back door, pausing before she entered the house. "How is Priya?"

"She won't talk to me. Neither of them are talking. Could you come here to the school?"

Annette entered the house. "Yes, of course."

∗　∗　∗

Drew didn't agree with the accommodations Elizabeth had chosen. *The Strathallan? What the fuck are you thinking?* The place was too upscale, and they needed to be under the radar. He even asked if she was feeling okay. Elizabeth told him to pull down his hat where it belonged and to get their suitcases. They checked in just fine. Elizabeth put on her charm, snuggling up to Drew and acting the love-stricken fiancé. He played along as he handed over his credit card. Elizabeth nuzzled his neck and flashed a diamond ring at the front desk clerk.

"That's a beautiful ring."

"Thank you. He spoils me."

"Nothing but the best for my girl." Drew smiled at the clerk until she turned her back. He glared at Elizabeth then at the ring. The clerk turned around with their key, and the smile returned to Drew's face.

Elizabeth kept the act up as they went to their room. She hung on him. She kissed him. She grabbed his ass. Drew unlocked the door and ushered his handsy fake fiancé inside. Elizabeth walked to the mini bar and opened the bottle of tequila. Drew dropped their suitcases and rushed to her, grabbing the liquor from her hands.

"What the fuck, Lizzie?"

"I was going to drink that."

"No," he said as he guzzled the contents. "You're not." He walked to her and grabbed her left hand, glaring at the ring and back to her. "Collecting trophies now? The scalp wasn't good enough? And this place? Since when do we stay in a place like this? Under the radar. Under the radar." Drew stormed to the mini bar, opened another bottle of tequila, slammed the contents, and tossed the bottle in the trash. "Do you know how much a place like this costs?"

"I pay the bills so what does it matter?"

"Are you hearing yourself right now? All of this matters."

"Well, I'm tired of crappy hotel rooms with god-knows-whats crawling on the beds."

"Not like it would affect you. You can't die."

"You're right. Almost. You'd have to cut off my head, but that would pretty much kill anything." Elizabeth tore off her clothes.

Drew looked away holding his hands to his face. "What the fuck, Lizzie."

"Relax, I'm just getting in the shower."

*   *   *

Elizabeth took a long, hot shower. She toweled off, quietly opened the door, and tiptoed into their room. She saw Drew passed out fully clothed on top of the bed. Elizabeth smiled as she reached in her bag. She looked at the diamond that sparkled on her finger. The ring wasn't the only thing she'd purloined. Elizabeth had to admit, the last kill had style.

She took the hotel shuttle to the closest dive bar. She asked to be taken to a "dive" bar. Tonight called for tequila, and she would have her tequila, Drew be damned. Patrón Gold was just the thing to soothe her nerves. After three shots down, it was time to hustle. She started at the dart board. The men flocked to her, offering to teach her a good game. She stood in her tight black dress and high heels teaching them a thing or two instead. She bought rounds with her winnings. A sore loser came back into the bar.

"Hey, bitch. You played me," he said to Elizabeth.

"Nope." Elizabeth slammed another shot of tequila. "I just play better. You should see me at pool."

He stood next to her. His baseball cap hung over his eyes. He grabbed her by the wrist and swung her around in the bar stool. "I don't like getting hustled, especially by some glam twat."

Elizabeth pushed him to the floor. She slid off her stool. "And I don't like being touched." She kicked him in the ribs. "Here's a thought. Learn your game." She kicked him again cracking his ribs. "Come on, stud. You wanted to get it on when you saw me." She stood on his balls listening to him moan in pain. "Well, now's your chance, asshole."

Elizabeth felt herself lifted off the ground and slammed against the bar. "Been lookin all over for you. Think you've had enough fun for tonight," Drew growled. Baseball Cap was still moaning on the floor. Drew dug in his pocket and threw some money at him. "Sorry man. This one can't drink. No harm meant."

"Screw you," the man said, clutching his groin.

Elizabeth pushed at Drew. "I'm not ready to go."

Drew pulled her up and dragged her towards the door. "Sorry folks. Don't worry, we won't be back."

*   *   *

Elizabeth sat on the bed, watching Drew as he paced the hotel room. Megadeth blasted from his boombox. He slammed a beer, threw the can in the trash, and cracked open another one.

"Can I get one of those?"

"No." He threw his hat against the wall and kept pacing.

Elizabeth hated his music and couldn't stand his fidgeting. She got up, placed her hands on his flushed cheeks, and looked into his green eyes. "Aren't you a bit young to be listening to Megadeth? I always pictured you as a 21 Pilots kind of guy. I guess if you have to go old school, you could at least listen to GWAR. According to *Loudwire,* they're still relevant. I mean at least get rid of the boombox. I did buy you an iPhone."

Drew walked to his boombox and turned the volume up and kept pacing. Elizabeth got up and turned the music off. She stood in front of Drew and put her hands on his cheeks. "I'm sorry. You're right. I haven't been myself." Elizabeth kissed his cheeks then his lips.

Drew put his hand on her stomach and gently pushed away. "What are you doing?" he asked. "I'm your partner. That shit's not gonna work on me. It won't work on anyone." He flicked her silver necklace with the Chi Rho pendant hanging at her neck. "You can't get me hard. Hell, you can't get anyone hard." He guzzled more of his beer and pointed the can at her. "Your father made sure of that."

Elizabeth hated her pendant. Drew had one just like it. She couldn't remove it. Only Drew could do that, something Drew wouldn't do, as it meant certain death for him or any male around. This symbol safeguarded the bearer from the magic of the succubus, but it also made sure Elizabeth remained chaste. As much as she wanted to break free of its protection, she couldn't. So, from time to time, to blow off steam, Elizabeth picked a fight. Decades of pent-up sexual energy found its way out through smashing in the occasional man's face. It was the only way Elizabeth knew how to cope. Drew was the only man who hadn't quit the assignment; he was the only one who had lasted longer than a month. "I don't need you," Elizabeth said and walked away from him. She lay on the bed, turning away from him.

"By all rights, I should cut your head off, but you're the only one who can find your insane mother. You're making my job really difficult right now." He pulled a chair next to the bed and tapped Elizabeth on the shoulder.

She was still angry, still ready to punch, kick, or bite something. She pushed those emotions down where all her other emotions tried to hide and turned to her partner.

Drew grew quiet. "For some insane reason, I like you. So, before you go to sleep, not that I believe that you really sleep, but, before you close your eyes and do whatever it is that you do, it's time for a story. I had a friend. My best friend. Hell, the only friend I ever had. His name was Oscar, and I loved him."

"Where did you meet Oscar?"

"Pet store."

"So, Oscar was your pet dog?"

"Turtle, a red slider. Oh, he was great. I could tell Oscar anything. I didn't have parents to talk to. Lived with my grandpa after they died. New school, new teachers, new bullies, but Oscar was always there for me." Drew went to the small fridge and grabbed another beer. "But then one morning, Oscar stopped moving. I stroked his shell and waited for him to poke his little head out. Nothing. Worst day of my life. Me and my grandpa buried him under the birch tree in the back yard. I always swore that when I died I'd be buried there with him. With Oscar."

"Why are you telling me this?"

"Who's your friend? I admit, me and Oscar—pretty pathetic—but at least I had him." He paused. "So, who's *your* friend? Who's *your* Oscar?"

"I've had plenty friends."

"Really? Because all I see is a bunch of enemies. Everywhere we go, you pick a fight. You're not happy until you get blood on your clothes. You want us to hunt these women. These women who are just like you, and yet you act worse than any woman I've ever seen."

"And you think it's easy for me? I try to do the right thing, but I have all this—this energy—I haven't had sex in sixty-two years. And I still can't. So, what do you suppose I do? Sit here and watch you sleep?"

"Sixty-two? So, you *have* had sex. I'm sorry, but I just assumed that you were a virgin."

"Well, I'm not."

"That changes everything, don't you think?"

"I thought we were discussing best friends here," Elizabeth said. She got up and grabbed a beer from the fridge. Drew looked at her disapprovingly. "Don't," Elizabeth retorted as she cracked open the beer. She sat on the bed. Drew sat next to her.

"I did have someone," she said after a while. "Samuel. I knew him since I was a little girl and we did everything together." Elizabeth wiped at her eyes. There were no tears yet, but she felt them coming. "He was drafted for the Korean War. He asked me to marry him. We were at the beach, and the sun had just started to set. He was too poor to give me a ring, but I didn't care. I loved him." She looked up at the ceiling. "Of course, I said yes. We made love. It was my first time, but when I woke up he was dead. I ran home and told my father what had happened. He followed me to the beach, and that's when he told me what I was. What I could do. What I would do if I ever touched a man again.

"I went through Samuel's bag and grabbed his hunting knife. I threw it at my father's feet and told him to kill me. He wouldn't do it. He held me against his chest as I cried. That's when he told me about my mother, a full-fledged succubus. My father was a Catholic priest when she raped him. He left the church and considered suicide, which was what my mother hoped for, the eternal damnation of his soul. But when he didn't kill himself, she left me on his doorstep. My father lived because my mother allowed him to live. Samuel—he died because I loved him so much. I didn't grow up with my mother. I didn't know about this power or how to use it. She could control it. I can't."

"And the baby? Sorry, but with your kind, there's always a child."

"She's dead. My father took me to this place, a dirty and dank apartment, not the doctor's offices women go to now. Sometimes I can still feel them scraping my insides." Elizabeth looked at Drew.

"At times, I wish he had just killed me."

Drew set his beer on the nightstand, took off his shoes, and lay next to Elizabeth. She placed her head on the pillow as he pulled her close to him and caressed her flat stomach. "I'm sorry. I didn't know."

Elizabeth placed her hand over Drew's. "I guess you're my only friend now. Sorry I'm such a pain in your ass."

Drew kissed the back of her head. "Hey, what are friends for?"

*　*　*

Annette felt unusual aches and pains. She hadn't been sleeping well, plagued by the same dream night after night for the past four days. It was unusual for her to have dreams, much less remember them. Even this dream was on the brink of escaping her memory, but one image would not leave her: Priya's bloody head rolling down an alley. Someone was in the alley, but Annette couldn't see who it was. Maybe it was Annette in the alley. Maybe the murderer was her. Oh God, did Annette hate her daughter that much? Maybe she should see her shrink again.

She needed to get out of her house. There was nothing left to clean, no more yard work to be completed. It had been a while since Annette photographed anything of substance. Annette quickly dressed, purse on her shoulder and camera in hand.

She listened to Led Zeppelin as she drove to East Avenue. Usually the music relaxed her, but her dream haunted her. Her daughter's latest outburst against that boy bothered her. All she knew was that the boy's name was Brian, and for some reason, Priya was furious with him. *Did he touch you, honey? Did you have sex with him? You can tell me.* The well-intended questions just infuriated her daughter further. Priya had picked up a vase which held a beautiful arrangement of peach roses and baby's breath. She threw it across the room. The vase exploded against the wall, leaving a shard of glass in Annette's cheek. Priya stood up and kicked the stool she had been sitting on. *You don't get it. You'll never get it.*

Annette pulled over and cried. Her hands gripped the steering wheel. Zeppelin's "Kashmir" blasted through the speakers. She missed her college pal Kevin and wished she could call him. Steven made it very clear before they got married: no male friends. Kevin was the only one who got her. She didn't know how to reach him, not after all these years.

Annette looked up from her steering wheel. Before her breakdown she had been aimlessly driving around. She looked at the street sign: *East Avenue.* Her camera was on the seat next to her, ready to capture the artsy yuppies walking in and out of old mansions turned into businesses. She wiped the tears from her eyes and decided to indulge her camera's hunger to capture life's moments in action. She locked her wallet in the glove box, grabbed her camera, and walked into the busy sidewalk.

There was a structure across the street that hadn't been there before. She could have sworn it should have been a bank. It was modern in style. She had to get a picture of the glass and metal structure sitting here at odds with the brick and mortar surrounding it. Her camera seemed to move for her—click, click, snap, snap, snap: capture. She was nothing more than the pressure needed to push the button and kidnap the scene set before her. She wanted to get inside. She felt a sense of guilt as she walked up the sidewalk to knock on the front door. No answer. Annette retreated and decided to check out the back of the building. There was no one there to pitch a stink.

An alley led to the back. Annette continued taking pictures as she proceeded down the slate walkway. When she focused her camera on the building, she noticed strange symbols scribbled on the side.

Annette pulled her camera away from her face. She looked at the building. There were no symbols. "Weird."

"Can I help you?"

Annette jumped, startled by the voice. How long had he been standing there watching her intrude on the property? At first, Annette was angered, but then she realized that she was the one in the wrong. She turned and saw a short, portly man standing in the alley behind her. She held her camera to her chest and tried to catch her breath.

The man looked at her camera. "Are you from the paper? They said they weren't coming until tomorrow."

"Uh, no. I just love this building," Annette said. "I didn't mean to intrude."

"Oh, thank you." The man was short, like Danny DeVito short. In a way, he acted like Danny DeVito. "We're opening soon. I thought maybe you were from the paper."

"No, just taking pictures. What is it that you're opening?" Annette felt her towering presence over him, yet the way he acted made her feel so paltry.

"A restaurant." He turned and walked toward the street.

Annette dug in her pocket and grabbed her keys. "A restaurant? I didn't see an advertisement for a new restaurant? What kind of restaurant?"

"Maybe you *should* be working for the paper," the man scoffed. "It will be a fine dining experience suited to the needs of selective patrons. Exquisite." His voice was raspy, just like DeVito. Was she talking to fucking Danny DeVito? "We open in two days," he continued, "but I could let you peek inside."

Annette didn't trust his smile or the way this short man who wanted to give her a private tour looked at her. She pretended to check her watch. "Thank you, but I can't. I have to pick up my daughter," she lied.

"Too bad. At least let me give you my card. I'm Benny. Come back for our opening and give the host the card. You'll be taken care of."

"Wow, thanks." She tucked the card in her pants pocket. "I'm Annette, by the way."

"I look forward to seeing you and your daughter at our opening. Oh, and bring those pictures if you don't mind. Can't always trust the paper to get that perfect shot."

* * *

You could hear Priya's stereo blasting from the driveway. Annette walked inside, threw her keys on the coffee table, and walked upstairs. Usually she knocked. But not this time. The music was making the walls shake. Annette pushed open her daughter's door. Priya was on her bed, crumpled snot-filled tissues strewn on the comforter. Annette turned the volume down on the stereo and sat next to her daughter.

"I was listening to that," Priya said.

"You and the entire neighborhood."

"What do you want, Annette?"

Annette reached over and brushed Priya's hair from her face. She looked into her daughter's tear-drenched eyes. Streaks from her mascara ran down her cheeks. Her eyes were swollen. Her skin felt hot. "I just want..." Annette touched Priya's hair. "I want to help you."

"When will Daddy be back?" Priya pushed her mother's hand away and sat up. Annette sat next to her in silence. Priya brushed the tears from her cheeks. "You want to help me? Tell me when he'll be back."

"Ten days."

Priya jumped off the bed and turned the volume up on the stereo. "That's great. So, I'm stuck with you."

"Talk to me. We used to talk all the time. I'm your—"

"Don't you dare say it, because you're not. And now Daddy's gone, but you—you probably drove him away. You sent him away from me." Priya stomped on the floor and pulled at her hair. Annette ran to her daughter and grabbed her wrist trying to keep her from pulling out more hair.

"Get off me," Priya said as she shoved Annette to the floor. "You drove him away, and I need him now. Billy won't talk to me, because I couldn't do it. Daddy knew what to do. He always knew. What do you know, Annette? How to keep a house clean? Or are you taking your pathetic pictures again?" She walked to her bedroom window and traced the curtain with her fingers.

"Couldn't do what? Priya, what did this boy want you to do?"

"Nothing. It doesn't matter. None of it matters."

"No, Sweetie, it does matter. What you are feeling matters. What did this boy do to you?"

"I couldn't be with him, because he wasn't like Daddy. He

could never love me the way Daddy loves me. The whole school thinks we did, but we didn't. And now Daddy's gone. But what does it matter now? He's gone." Priya grabbed the hairbrush from her vanity and threw it at Annette. "It's all your fault. He loves me more than he would ever love you. I know Daddy still loves me, and you sent him away from me," Priya huffed and collapsed to the floor.

It came together. The way he favored her. The way he dismissed her outbursts. The way he refused to look at Annette and the attention he showered on Priya. "No, your father wouldn't. He couldn't." Annette could not move. She watched Priya sob, sniffling snot across her sleeve. Annette wanted to grab her daughter and wrap her arms around her. She wanted to tell her little girl that she would make everything right. But her muscles stiffened. She was frozen. Something should blink, because all she could do was stand there wide eyed and comatose.

* * *

Elizabeth held the leathered scalp in her hand and studied the map burned into its skin. "Turn left up ahead. The street should be coming up in about a mile, on the right."

"I need some tunes," Drew said.

"No." Elizabeth blocked his hand from the stereo. "I don't want them to hear us coming."

"And a quiet car driving slowly by is supposed to be inconspicuous? Come on, everyone has music blasting in their cars." He brushed her hand aside and turned on the car stereo. Harry

Styles' "Sign of the Times" blared through the speakers. He smiled as he made a left-hand turn. "Figured you're tired of my metal."

"Yeah," Elizabeth said. "This is *so* much better. Your metal made me want to kill someone, maybe now I'll just slit my own wrists." Elizabeth looked at Drew, who was smiling. He reached over and grabbed her hand. Elizabeth felt she should have withdrawn her hand from his touch, but she remained still as he rubbed her fingers. "You're gonna stay on this street for a while."

Drew looked at the scalp. He looked at Elizabeth. "Does it ever bother you?"

"Does what bother me?" she asked. She could feel the heat coming from his fingers. The pendants protected him, but what did they do for her? Here they were in a car searching for their next mark, and all the while Harry Styles filled the car as Drew caressed her hand. Did the pendants protect her from his seduction?

Drew rounded the corner. "You're hunting these women, some of them girls."

"And?"

"And. They're like you. You kill your own kind. I would've thought you'd be happy to find them."

"Oh, I *am* happy to find them—with each one I scalp I get closer to her." Elizabeth looked back at the map. "It should be coming up soon. Park up there."

"And once you find them all, once you find and kill your mother, then what?" He gripped her hand as he parked the car.

"I kill myself," Elizabeth said.

He pulled the key from the ignition and turned to her. "So, you will chop your own head off. How will that work? Let me guess, you'll need some assistance."

"Of course."

"And I'm to be your assistance."

"If you live that long. Yes." Elizabeth finally withdrew her hand. She felt uncomfortable with the way Drew was looking at her. His gray eyes peered into her, questioning her demand for extermination. She looked at her feet then said, "It's what you signed up for. It's why I'm paying you." Elizabeth looked back at Drew. "That was part of your instructions. Once this is over, you have to kill me. End the line."

Drew looked away from her. He put the car keys in his pocket. "We should check this place out." He reached for the door.

Elizabeth grabbed his arm. "Can you not do this? Let me know now."

"I can do it," Drew said. They got out of the car and looked at the building the scalp map led them to. "Uh, it not a house." He turned to her. "It's a restaurant of some sort."

"That's strange."

"What's going on with that map? According to the sign, this place doesn't even open for two more days. So now what?" Drew pulled his hat off and began crumpling it in his hands.

"We come back."

Annette hoped taking Priya to Benny's restaurant would cheer her daughter up, but all Priya did was push her food around her plate. "When's Daddy coming home?" Priya didn't even look at her mother as those words exited her lips.

"We've been over this. Eight more days. Annette drank her martini and motioned the waitress for another one.

"You really shouldn't drink so much." Priya let her fork drop to her plate.

"Can we not do this now?"

"Right. My mistake. Mother and daughter bonding time. Except, you're not my mother."

Annette smoothed the napkin on her lap. "I am your mother. I carried you. I nourished you."

"Yeah. You did all that. But your eggs were too rotten to make me. You had to go to one of those banks designed for desperate women who want to keep their husbands. Here's the waitress with your martini." Priya stood up. "I have to go throw up now."

*　*　*

Elizabeth snickered when Drew opened the door for her. "Gotta look the part," he said pointing to the new duds Elizabeth bought for him. "Oh, but you look great too. Get the table. I gotta hit the head."

"My Lancelot"

"Huh?"

"Never mind." Elizabeth checked in with the hostess as Drew

looked for the restrooms. "Two for dinner please," Elizabeth said.

"Do you have a reservation?"

"No. Surely you can fit two in for dinner."

"Tonight is a closed event. Reservations only. I'm sorry."

Elizabeth gripped her black clutch. A short, fat man pushed through the crowd gathered at the hostess stand. "Zoe, this woman is on the list. See, right there," he said pointing to the computer." The man looked up from the glaring light of the computer and smiled. "Zoe will show you to your table." Elizabeth smiled back finally recognizing not so much the man, but the energy that emanated from him.

Elizabeth followed the hostess to the table ordered a beer for Drew and an iced tea for herself. Fifteen minutes went by. She wondered what could be keeping him. She saw a woman tapping the side of her martini glass with her fingernail. The woman looked around the room, threw her napkin on the table, and stormed off to the bathroom.

"Priya?" the woman called. "Priya?" She came back to the dining room and looked around. She ran back to the bathrooms. Elizabeth heard a door open and slam shut. "Priya?" The woman's voice grew distant as if she was now outside.

Elizabeth stood up and wanted to follow the woman. She wanted to know where Drew was. The whole situation was unnerving to her, to be in a restaurant instead of a dwelling space with a clear target to pursue. The same portly man from the hostess stand approached her table.

"Come with me," he said in a low voice, grabbing her by the arm. Elizabeth tried to yank her arm away in vain. "Let's not make a scene, not on my opening night."

Elizabeth stood and followed him to an office in the kitchen. He pushed her into a chair that sat opposite a large metal desk.

"Behemoth," she sneered.

"Call me Benny. Behemoth is so archaic, don't you think?" He stood against the office door. Elizabeth reached to the sides of her thighs, reaching into the holster, and gripped her knives. "Those blades won't work on me and you know it. It's not my head you're after."

"My partner's out there. I need to get to him." She withdrew her hands from the black lace holsters.

"Oh," he giggled. "No. Not show time yet. So nice of you to dress up for my little venue, not your usual beheading garb."

"It's a swanky place. I needed to blend."

"Blend? You? Never, but you're here."

"Your point?"

"I'm afraid your mother has been very busy with certain donor banks." Benny sat at his desk, opened, a drawer and pulled out a bottle of Kilbeggan Irish whiskey. He pulled out two shot glasses and poured. He offered Elizabeth a glass. She declined. "Ah, keeping the clear head."

"How many children are there?" Elizabeth asked.

"Born, probably a couple hundred. In the banks a few thousand. I guess you'll have to live a bit longer, won't you." Benny chuckled.

He drank the first shot.

"Why are you telling me this? Why help me?"

"I'm not helping you with any of this. I just thought you should know before you track down mommy dearest and kill yourself. There are more of these bitches out there than you know," he said. "Don't get me wrong, a succubus can be entertaining, but they're overstepping the boundaries. What am I supposed to do when all the men have been fucked into oblivion?" He stopped talking and listened. "Now it's show time."

"What do you mean?"

"Your partner. He'll be screaming. In three. Two. One." He drank the second shot. "Now you should run."

Elizabeth found Drew staggering down an alley behind the restaurant. He braced himself against the walls as he tried to walk back to the car.

"You're okay." Elizabeth rushed to his side.

"I wouldn't say that. I was coming out of the bathroom when this chick grabbed me. Some young firecracker. Bitch stabbed me." He dropped a steak knife. "I managed to get it away from her. I wouldn't kiss her. I think I ran into our girl." Drew slid to the ground. "Do me a favor and cut her head off."

"Jesus, you're losing so much blood." Elizabeth pulled off her wrap and tied it around Drew's waist.

"The mother ran after her."

Elizabeth kissed his forehead. His eyes fluttered shut. "Don't you do it," she said. "I'm the one who dies. Not you." She kissed him again. "I'll be back."

Elizabeth found a woman lying against the dumpster. Her dress was ripped to shreds as blood flowed ceaselessly from her belly. There was a rattle of bottles followed by a sob echoing farther down the alleyway. Elizabeth lifted her blades. A hand reached out and grabbed her by the ankle. Elizabeth swung around.

"You." The woman coughed up blood. "You leave my daughter alone."

"She's not your daughter."

"I know that." Annette's eyes fluttered closed. She opened them and tried to catch her breath. "But she's all I have left."

"Then I feel sorry for you." Elizabeth brushed the dying woman's hand away from her and continued down the alley. The target was in her sight. She thought of Drew and the poor woman butchered in the alley. This thing, this unwanted sibling would die tonight.

"You." Priya walked out of a doorway into the middle of the alley. There was a chain link fence behind her blocking the alley from the main road.

"Me," Elizabeth said.

"I felt you. Saw you in my dreams coming for me. I don't understand."

Elizabeth looked back at the dying woman then back to Priya. "I think you know why."

"Oh, Annette? She's nothing."

"She gave you life, and you took hers." Elizabeth kept

approaching Priya.

"My father gave me life, not that bag of bones over there."

"Regardless, this ends now."

Priya turned and jumped up the chain link fence. Elizabeth threw one of her blades, landing it in Priya's back. Priya fell onto the pavement on the other side of the fence. She pulled the knife from her back and pushed herself to her feet. "That hurt. Think I'll keep this as a souvenir. You should check on your man. I don't think he's gonna make it."

Elizabeth wanted to chase her, but she couldn't leave Drew to die. She watched Priya as she hobbled across the street and disappeared behind a building.

Drew was hunched over. "I'll get you to a hospital," Elizabeth said, pulling him to his feet.

"And say what?" He started to wheeze as he held the wound in his stomach. "I'm not gonna make it. Just get me out of here." He looked at Elizabeth. "Don't let me die here."

"Agreed."

Elizabeth sped down Route 104 and pulled over at a field. The farmhouse was boarded up, weeds twisting around the steps leading to the house. Drew looked out the window and smiled. "You found it. You found Oscar."

"What are friends for?" She got out of the car and looked at the old birch tree. It wasn't Oscar's tree, but to Drew it was, and that was all that mattered right now. She opened his door and started to lift him from the car. He pushed her away, insisting on walking, but he fell to the gravel driveway. Elizabeth hoisted him up.

"I wish I was strong like you. Beautiful and strong," he said.

"And tortured. You forgot tortured." She helped him to the tree and laid him gently on the moss-covered ground.

"I love you," he said.

"You're delirious." She lay next to him, her head on his chest, and listened to his weak heartbeat.

"You know why I couldn't kiss that girl? She wasn't you." Drew ripped the necklace from her neck. "Why be tortured?" Drew pulled Elizabeth on top of him. He pulled off his necklace. Despite the pain, he felt a surge of arousal. "I'm gonna die anyways."

UNDONE

Paige didn't want to go to the bathroom. She didn't want to see it again. True, she could just avert her eyes, but her mind would still know that it was there. Her head would shake. Her neck would ache as she felt her gaze pulled to the stain on the bottom of her porcelain tub. Something always drew her to that stain. There was another bathroom in her house, but whenever she had to pee, Michael was always in there. So, she was forced to use the upstairs bathroom and forced to look at that stain she just couldn't get rid of. Secretly she hated Michael for that, always hogging up the downstairs bathroom. Making her use the bathroom in their master suite. In fact, Paige noticed that most of Michael's belongings were no longer in the upstairs bathroom. His green scrubby still hung on the hook, but his shampoo and conditioner were gone. His Axe body wash was also gone. Razor? Gone. Toothbrush, still there, but Paige saw in the downstairs bathroom he had bought another toothbrush and new toothpaste. Michael never used the bathroom off their master suite anymore.

His sleeping patterns had changed as well. Paige often found herself waking up in the middle of the night alone. She would put on her bathrobe and tiptoe around the house looking for him. There he would be, asleep on the couch with a small blanket barely covering him. Paige didn't want to disturb him. She would lift the cover and tuck it under his toes. She would feel a tear fall from her eye and wipe it away. Was it something that she did? Maybe something she said? The distance. The coldness. The utter lack of communication. She knew she had to deal with the stain in the tub. She had tried everything. She was a good wife. She wanted to be a good mother, but that stain said otherwise. *Look at you. You can't even clean up a tub.* Paige tried all the cleaners. Those scrubbing bubbles she loved as a kid. Nope. Not sparkling and shining. She then tried bleach. Sealed the drain and poured three bottles in the tub. The stench of toxic chemicals filled the house. Paige opened the windows and fell asleep with rubber gloves on her hands. Nothing. The stains were still there, and Michael was furious when he came home from work. The house was rank with chemicals and the air frigid from the February winds of Upstate New York. Paige didn't bother an attempt to snuggle with Michael. She merely waited for him to fall asleep and covered up his feet with his blanket.

Yet here it was calling again. Her bladder and that bathroom. Paige stood up from her bed and stomped into the bathroom. She ran the sink. Usually she only did that when she had to defecate, but she ran the sink to just make noise. She hummed a song in her head. At first, she didn't recognize the humming of the song, but it all pulled together. Tori Amos "Liquid Diamonds." She sat on the toilet to pee. Nothing came out. She heard the water rush from the sink, but nothing from her came out. The shower curtains were pulled shut, but she could almost see that stain on the tub. Paige sat on the toilet with her mouth open. She stared at the floor. "I'm sorry," she said as the tears fought against her lower lids. She felt the moisture on her eyelashes then she felt them fall, all those tears. Her lashes felt a sense of relief as the liquid of pain fell from her face. She fell to her knees. She ripped open the shower curtain. She opened the cupboard under the sink and pulled out a bottle of Liquid-Plumr. She poured it in the tub. She saw the stain. She reached into the tub and punched the stain. She clawed the stain. She jumped in the tub and rubbed her half naked body against it.

Paige heard Michael stir downstairs. He was fighting his sleep. She could hear him shake on the couch and kick off his covers. She heard him stand up. She could see him rub his fingers through his hair then finally pull at his beard. Paige heard Michael come up the stairs. He entered the bathroom and sat on the side of the tub. He pulled the curtain back. His eyes were closed at first. Paige looked up at him. Would he finally see her? Michael held his face and began to sob. Paige wanted to jump up from the tub. She wanted to hit him in his face. *Look at me! See me! I'm here! Be my husband. I'm your wife.* She wanted to scream it, but all Paige could do was rock back and forth in the tub. All Paige could do was cry as she attempted to clean the stain. Michael reached into the tub. Paige felt Michael's hand pass through her ribcage as he touched the bottom of the tub.

"Damn soapstone tub," Michael said. "You insisted on it. And here it is. Still holding your blood in its pores."

BLUE LIPS

Lenora had always dreamed of being on a stage, with the bright lights, the cheering crowds, the velvet curtain, the makeup, and fancy costumes. Movies from her mother's youth fascinated her as well. As a little girl, she was to into all the old classics: *Breakfast at Tiffany's*, *The African Queen*, *Some Like It Hot*, and *Kiss Them for Me*. *One day,* she thought, *one day, I'm going to be a big star too.* She learned the lines, sat in front of the mirror, and practiced for her big break. But the theater stage never accepted her, and directors politely told her, "No." After years of heartache, she wound up on a different stage entirely—and though it was full of bright lights, it lacked the esteem and recognition she desired.

Lenora's daydreaming collided with Daisy who was hurriedly putting on her coat. "Hey, where do you think you're going?" she asked as she tapped Daisy's shoulder.

"Gotta get that money girl. Do me a favor and go up for me."

"Not again. You know I gotta get that money too," Lenora said, imitating her. She turned, looked in the mirror, and pretended to fix her hair.

Daisy reached in her purse and drew out a wad of cash. She thumbed through the ones and fives until she saw a twenty. "Here," she said, handing Lenora a twenty. "And a couple lines when I get back."

"Fine. Don't take too long. I'm tired of thinking up excuses for you when management comes back here."

"I'll be quick."[1]

Lenora quickly exchanged her police outfit for a black corset and a short leopard print skirt. She grabbed her peacock feathered fans and headed up the dressing-room stairs for the stage. The lights were not the lights of Broadway; the jeering crowd of old men was not the civilized company she sought when she was a teenager. Her outfit showed off her ass and breasts, an outfit fit neither for the big screen nor for a play. But bills had to be paid, and she could no longer hold out for childish dreams.

Amazingly, in this dump of lost dreams and forgotten

---

[1] "Whore (hohr) n. a prostitute, a sexually immoral woman" Daisy encompassed the meaning of this word "whore." In 2004, she had sexual relations for monetary compensation with over 500 men. She had hoped to be a star in the pornography industry; unfortunately, her constant herpes outbreaks overshadowed any possibility to be employed within the business. To abate her desires to be filmed, Daisy often videotaped her sessions of sexual encounters and placed them on her website. She hoped to one day build a name for herself on the World Wide Web. She came from a lineage of proud prostitutes. Her mother, as well as her mother's mother, were also whores. Whenever Daisy found herself in judicial complications, her grandmother, Elsa, was quick to call her attorney, Berny Smites, whose family had represented Daisy's for generations.

daughters, Lenora got lucky. A man—not too old, but not a pup—approached her and handed her a hundred-dollar bill. *Come talk to me* was all he said. Lenora couldn't wait for the music to end.

She ran into the back and was greeted with a shot of Jack Daniels and a line that could give Scarface a heart attack. "I can't do all of that."

"So, keep it for later." Daisy was wiping herself off with baby wipes and discarding them in the trashcan. The other girls in the dressing room were glaring at her from behind open locker doors, their eyes screaming "slut" and "trick," but everyone in that club had done something at least once to earn some extra cash. The only difference was that Daisy didn't pose to be a good girl.

Lenora did a quarter of the line and dumped the rest of it in cellophane from a cigarette pack. Her mind was tormented about using the cellophane—coke always sticks to it—but there was so much of it that she didn't care about the little bit that would be stuck on its surface. "Thanks, Daisy," she said as she slammed the shot. Lenora scurried to change from her outfit into a long green evening gown. Someone like him would like a little mystery. Seeing her naked on stage was one thing, but when she would get him alone, she wanted to make the moment last as long as possible. The longer he waited, the more money he would spend.

"Why cover it all up?" Daisy was still working on her line, slapping her leg at the burning sensation of the cocaine against her used up nasal membrane.

"Cause, he's that kinda guy." [2] Lenora hosed herself down with body spray to cover the sweat and powdered her face.

"Ooo, get it girl. Get that cash."

The coke had hit, and Lenora's heart began to race. Her throat was tingling and numb. She would have to get another drink to gain some semblance of a balance. It was so much stronger than the usual shit Daisy shoved up her nose. She hoped it would wear off before she had to go home. David would be waiting for her. David would be watching her, purposefully staring at her pupils to see if she was high again.

He just didn't get it, what this job could do to a girl. Furthermore, Lenora knew that he didn't want to fully comprehend it. Even though David had met her in the club, and promised that he would never get jealous, he wound up acting like every other boyfriend she had ever had. Waiting up for her, looking through her phone for new contacts, questioning her about what she did to make so much money. After all, he knew what Daisy did to make her money, but then again, everyone knew.

Lenora tried to push the thoughts of David out of her head as

______

[2] There are different types of gentlemen who frequent a strip club: the bachelor, the broke college student, the sex/drug addict, and the man of power. The man of power may attend the bar for relaxation or he may desire an entertainer to turn the table and boss him around. There was one such man of power back in 1991 who visited the Fox's Den in Roanoke, Virginia. His name was Edward Taylor Esquire. He paid the stripper, Bambi, a large sum of money for her to beat him and torture him with nipple clamps. Of course, to Edward, this was not torture but pleasure; this secret pleasure of his gave him a heart attack, and he was pronounced dead by the paramedics who arrived fifteen minutes later.

she made her way to the customer. He was already seated; a black cane with a lion's head was hooked over the arm of the over-stuffed chair. She sat in the chair next to him. Even though this was a strip club, management had a strange rule that the strippers weren't allowed to sit on the customers' laps. Said it wasn't "ladylike." Lenora thought it was a stupid rule, except when a guy was completely disgusting. Then she always spoke of the club's rule, glad to have dodged away from a pervert wearing running pants. [3]

Lenora again pushed needless thoughts out of her head. This guy wasn't your typical pervert. No more thoughts about guys in running pants. No more thoughts of David checking her purse—David shaking her wondering what she did at the club behind the curtain of the champagne room. *I should just leave him*, she thought.

"Hello, lovely," the man said.

"Hello back." Lenora was going to have a good night. She would deal with David's complaining later, but for now—she had a job to do.

"I think we should have more privacy," the man from stage said. He lit a cigarette, the red tip encircled by cascading smoke. Lenora

---

[3] Gents, listen up. Strippers know what you are up to when you enter the strip club wearing sweat pants. They know that you are going commando. You wear these sweat pants and strippers hate the fact that you wear them. We know that immediately you will get a hard on, and that your goal is to get off. We also think that you are disgusting for jizzing in your pants even though you usually leave the club right away. Gross. You are gross.

smiled. This was no rock.[4]

Lenora sat in the oversized chair next to him enjoying a snifter of scotch. She appreciated the man's demeanor. Straight to the point. No endless chatter. "What did you have in mind?"

"One of the private rooms would work."

"That'll cost you."

"Order it up."

Lenora flagged down a waitress. "He'd like to order a bottle of Moet." She saw the man roll his eyes. "Sorry, it's the best this place has." Lenora stood up and held out her arm to lead him to the champagne room.

He wasn't interested in dancing, just talking. It didn't matter to Lenora; it was all the same amount to her. She learned his name was Vincent. "P" was all he gave her for his last name. Frankly, she was surprised that he even gave her the initial at all. He went on and on about beauty, about the classic style of dance, about how much Lenora possessed that style. Lenora sipped on the champagne and feigned undying interest. He didn't touch the bubbly, claiming that

---

[4] Rock: Stripper slang. An unflattering description of a customer who nurses his drinks, doesn't tip dancers on stage, and doesn't get lap dances. Rocks are also referred to as "gawkers." This was all too common in the strip club. Daisy called these clients "Fred." There was a client who came in the club and tipped Daisy very well. He kept tipping her at the table, making Daisy feel that this customer was going to spend big money on her. Fred did not. He kept her there for two hours, and Daisy missed out on other men who wanted dances. Fred was a leech. Notice how Lenora's client does not waste her time. He tips her on the stage with a large bill. This clues the dancer that he is worth her time, and that the client wants her to spend time with him. Also note how the client does not waste time with endless chatter. He goes right for what he wants, privacy with the stripper, with money to spend.

it was a drink for the ladies.

Vincent grabbed his wallet from his jacket and took out a card. Lenora peered at the card Vincent was holding. *Here we go. Another card to add to the pile of cards that I won't call. Even if I wanted to, I'm not allowed.* He handed it to Lenora and refilled her glass. Lenora looked at the card; it was silver in color with the writing embossed in a bright blue. "Blue Lips?" She accepted the glass of champagne. "What's this?"

"My club."[5]

"Never heard of it."

"It's private. Not many have. Anyway, I think you would be perfect for it. I run a classy establishment."

"Sounds strange."

"Stranger than this place. At our first encounter, you said you loved the classic movies: Jane Mansfield, Audrey Hepburn. I run a burlesque show not a seedy strip club." Vincent put his hands together as if in prayer.

"Yeah, I'll think about it."

Vincent stood up and drew five hundred from his wallet. He set

---

[5] Recruiting dancers while in another club is frowned upon. Often recruiters will take the dancer for a private dance. This is done for the recruiter to get a better look as well as to test the dancer's "skills." The recruiter may also want to see just how far the dancer will go. Not all recruiters want dirty girls, girls such as the lascivious Daisy. They preferred dancers such as Pamela Sinclaire. A recruiter from Dallas had spotted Miss Sinclaire in a small club outside of Biloxi, Mississippi. He brought her back to his club, Sensations, and in less than two weeks, the dancer was pulling in over 5,000 dollars a night. This, of course, brought the club enormous money all thanks to the recruiter.

it on the couch next to her. "For your time." He began to exit the room but stopped and turned. "Just think about it. We'd love to have you."

* * *

Vincent didn't like waiting. He was always the first in line, the first to have the latest trends, the first to make a buck, the first to get the girl. Two days had gone by and still no phone call from Lenora. Patience. Patience. Well, he had none. He sulked in his office, the music pumping outside. He should be happy that he was doing so well. It's not easy for a man his age to be in tune with the newest crazes. To give people what they wanted. But in the hundred fifty years in which he planned his ventures, one thing rang true. Men loved sex, and those with money would pay anything to furnish their darkest desires.

He grew tired of staring at the phone and decided to walk through the club. See who was in tonight. See how all his lovelies were doing. The club was packed again. Everyone seemed to be enjoying themselves. Veronica was on the swing, singing a lovely song. Mike was slinging drinks. Each customer had a beauty next to him, and the cash was pouring in. Vincent cradled the top of his cane as he limped towards the bar and sat down. His knee hadn't throbbed so painfully in decades.

"Hey-ya, Boss."

"Scotch." Vincent looked at his statues in the center of the club. Priceless artifacts out in the open. Persephone, Adonis,

Hermes, Ereshkigal, and Thoth[6]—their eyes, which usually glowed a brilliant blue, were fading. There was no amount of lighting that could disguise it, and the pain in his knee was getting worse by the minute.

"Sure thing," Mike said, grabbing the bottle of Glenlivet from the top shelf.

"Business looks good," Vincent said, accepting the drink. He swirled the ice cubes around in the glass before taking a sip. "But then again, when has it not been good?"

"All thanks to you."

"Hey, pour yourself some. You know how I hate drinking alone."

"Doesn't look like you'll have to," Mike said, pointing at the door.

Vincent turned and saw her. Finally, here. And in person. *How wonderful*, he thought. She made her way through the club to the bar.

"My, isn't this a surprise." Vincent stood and offered Lenora a hug. "Have a seat."

"Thanks, sorry I didn't call. I was a bit tied up."

"But you're here now. That's what matters."

"I must have misplaced the card, but I remembered where you said the place was. So, I decided to just come over and check it out."

---

[6] Little is known to the common people of these gods and goddesses. In the black arts, they are more than statues. They are real entities with the power to aid a practitioner in necromancy. Of course, a participant is required.

"Marvelous. Marvelous, really. Care for a drink?"

"Of course."

"Mike, give the lady whatever she wants," he said. He nodded to Lenora. "Then I'll give you the tour."

Lenora got more than a tour. She was amazed at the stage, so elaborate with the clear glass floors and the blue flashing lights. It almost appeared as if the girls were gliding on pure oceanic waves. There was even a velvet curtain, but this was a blue curtain—not the crimson curtain she had craved. There was a girl in a swing, and even props for a silk rope show.[7]

"Oh my God, I've always wanted to do an aerial silk rope show. I learned how to do it, but these clubs weren't willing to install the equipment. Said it wasn't what the clientele was looking for," she gushed.

"You will." Vincent patted her shoulder and kept the tour going.

The whole thing was set up more as a cabaret of sorts rather than a stuffy strip club, where only one thing was expected: the bearing of tits and ass for the clientele to see. Some of the performers didn't remove their clothes at all. Here bigger wasn't better. What was important was talent. Some sang. Some recited poetry—although Lenora thought the verse was a bit morbid at times. It was a hodge-podge of talent wrapped up in beauty. Lenora

---

[7] Artists of this craft use their skill to perform aerial acrobatics without the aid of safety harnesses. This performance art is believed to have been started in 1959 by a French circus, and became a global sensation through Cirque du Soleil by 1995.

wanted in. The only thing that bothered her was the fact that it was so damn cold. Better to deal with the physical discomfort of chilliness than the coldness of her relationship. To hell with him. To hell with David. To hell with his fucking cat. Lenora was not a cat person as much as she tried to be. She felt that Mrs. Knibbles knew this. She was always looking at her in her cross-eyed Siamese way. She was just waiting for the damn furball to take a bite out of her one of these nights and end it all. End the woman who had come between the feline and her owner. She was so glad that the bastard had finally fallen asleep. It was then that she stole away. It was then that she decided to leave everything he represented behind.

"Vincent, it's amazing."

"So, you'll join our little show?"

"In a heartbeat."

"Fabulous. We just need to go over some paperwork." Vincent led her towards the back of the building and through two heavy double doors. These doors weren't see-through like the rest of the club, but rather made of brilliant cherry wood with ornate flowered door knobs. They opened into a dimly lit hallway. Lenora had to squint so she wouldn't trip on the carpeted floor. She held on to Vincent's arm, as he led her into his office.

She sat in a chair opposite Vincent at his desk. There were pictures everywhere. Pictures of beautiful women cast in watercolor and oil paint. Behind her there was a heavy curtain. She wanted to pull the curtain back and see what treasure he had hidden there, but Lenora decided to squash her curiosity and get on with the paperwork.

The rules were pretty normal. She couldn't work for another establishment. Had to give a schedule. Wasn't allowed to leave with the customers. *Probably why he didn't approach Daisy*, Lenora thought, smiling to herself.

Vincent caught the smile. "What is it?" he asked setting the paperwork aside.

"Oh, it's just that I always had dreams of a stage. Granted this isn't exactly what I was searching for, but it's definitely a nice change."

Vincent smiled. He sat there looking at her and smiling. Lenora fiddled with her skirt. "Oh, one more thing."

"Yes?"

"I couldn't help but notice your curiosity." Vincent stood up and limped to the curtain. "Would you like to take a peek?"

"I didn't mean to be rude."

"No rudeness at all. It's a piece I've been working on. I would love for you to tell me what you think." He waved his hands around the room. "I dabble in the arts. So, could you give me your honest opinion?"

"Of course." Lenora was embarrassed. Of course, she was excited to see his hidden work of art, but she was no art aficionado. She was a stripper. She didn't want to blow it. Didn't want Vincent to change his mind about her. What if she wasn't good enough to be in his club? She watched as his hands clutched the side of the curtain. He pulled the curtain back. For once, Lenora was happy that she didn't have cocaine running through her veins to add to this crazy trip.

At first, she couldn't see anything. There was no immediate work of art, but rather another room entirely. There were candles lit that burned an iridescent blue. She felt a tingling in her fingertips and toes, an apprehension of moving a step closer.

Vincent beckoned. "Well, go ahead my dear. I do apologize for the lighting, but it is what I think makes this piece so inspiring."

Lenora wanted to pull back, wanted to run from the room, but her feet wouldn't obey her. She walked closer to Vincent, closer to the curtain, closer to the flickering flames of blue. She arrived in the center of the room, and Vincent was right behind her with his hand lightly nudging her by the small of her back. She saw no work of art. No painting. No sculpture, but rather a bed. There was something in the bed. She couldn't quite make it out, but it appeared to be a female. Lenora tried to step back, but Vincent forced her to the bed. She let out a yelp as she fell, tumbling in airy taffeta white sheets, surrounded by blue light.

"You really have to get up close to admire her." Vincent stepped back as Lenora was enwrapped in bony arms, flesh barely holding on to the skeleton of the creature's frame. She felt teeth puncture her flesh repeatedly. "She's really quite something. Quite a beauty in her day. Men kneeled at the sight of her, but she was my Duchess. Mine and mine alone."[8]

---

[8] There is a rumor that The Duchess of Malfi was based on a real character, but the ending of

Lenora's screams were trapped in the taffeta, trapped in the arms of the Duchess, whose flesh was becoming fuller, more defined with every bite she took. "Vincent," the Duchess whispered. Lenora felt her bloody teeth at her ear.

"Oh, my darling." Vincent swooned, holding his hands to his chest. He looked to Lenora and smiled. "We were married in secret, but I wasn't exactly in the proper aristocratic circle for such a union. They murdered her, took her from me." Lenora watched in horror as Vincent pulled a knife from his inner coat pocket. "They damned her, but I found a way to make her live. Live with me always." Vincent grabbed Lenora by the hair and slit her throat. Her blood flowed over the sheets, soaking the bed, then disappeared into the cat statues underneath.

"It's done now, my sweet," he said as he lay on the bed next to his Duchess. Soon you'll be as you always were."

"And so will you." The Duchess pushed Vincent on his back and quickly began unbuttoning his clothes.

"Not yet," Vincent said, kissing her.

"No, now." She attempted to force him back down, but her body was still so weak.

"The statues, and let's not forget the beauty who gave her life for us."

---

that tragic revenge play had been altered to keep the true horror of that piece of history hidden from the world. The Duchess indeed survived her fate at the hands of her brother. Her lover was not slain, but instead turned to the Black Arts to revive his lover and keep her with him forever.

"Minor details," the Duchess said, licking his face with her half-formed tongue.

"Details which cannot be forsaken." Vincent stood up and straightened his blood-soaked jacket.

"Come back to me." Even now Vincent could see his lover gain strength. The definition around her legs was back; her breasts were full and plump again; her hair had regained its long and thick length.

"I always do." He kissed her hands which were forming so quickly now—from skeletal remains back to the youthful fingertips that had accepted the ring she had provided. "I always do."

*   *   *

David sat at the bar turning the card between his fingers. He didn't like the feel of this place. For one, it was too damn cold. The bar was inlaid with metal which had frosted ice for the customers to set their drinks to keep them chilled. Everything had blue lighting, and the fixtures were clear as if imitating glass or ice. Nothing seemed comfortable. Even his chair was hard. *Strange, strange place.* David called the bartender over to order a drink.

A tall, gangly man sat in the stool next to him, eyeing him over and over. The bartender nodded in recognition and poured the regular a gin and tonic. "You look new," the man said. "Come here to crack open a cold one?"

"Something like that," David said as the bartender set a bottle of Amstel on the bar.

"Well, I tell ya, once you get a taste of this place, you'll never stop coming. Ain't nothing like it. Things happen here that you never thought were possible."

"Thanks for the tip." David grabbed his beer and walked away from the guy. The more he talked, the angrier David became. Just the thought of Lenora working here disgusted him. He didn't know why. The club was definitely classier than the other place, but there was a strange vibe here. The girls were pretty, but they all were dressed in white and wearing the same strange blue makeup. Even their skin had a glittery blue hue to it. Besides, Lenora promised him she'd get out of the game, now that he was making enough money for both of them. Two days. He hadn't seen her in two days. All he had to go by was this card stashed in the hiding spot for her cocaine. Yeah, another thing she was supposed to have quit.

David hadn't seen her yet, but he was convinced that she was here. No matter how he pleaded with her to get out of this shit, he had a feeling that she would always be a stripper.[9] There were so many girls here, there'd be no telling when she would be on stage. He decided to sit on the floor. There were statues of what David guessed to be old goddesses and gods standing in every corner of the club. They all seemed to be watching the show with a strange and brilliant blue light flowing out of their sockets as if they were all a version of a sphinx. Maybe they were all looking at him, looking

---

[9] Unfortunately, strippers rarely have healthy relationships, especially those relating to love. As much as boyfriends say they can handle their woman taking her clothes off for money, none rarely can.

into his heart. Was it truthful? Just? Right? David already knew the answer. Nope. Nope. Nope. He was a sinner. A sinner for dating a stripper. A sinner for tying her up in her bedroom. A sinner for coveting her, for not only wanting her, for not only wanting to be inside of her, but also for wanting to control her every move. To make her his. His property. And he had the gun to prove it. He knew she was here. Felt it, and she was going to leave with him one way or another. At first, David was a little nervous about bringing a gun in here, but for some reason, clubs of this kind don't search perverts. [10]

There was no DJ speaking over the microphone announcing the girls, and in between their acts there were bouts of deranged and perverse comedy. One actor ripped off a manikin's arm and beat her with it for not getting on her knees fast enough. Strange humor. A woman sang afterwards some strange melodramatic and eerie song. David didn't get it. The curtains opened again, revealing a woman suspended on blue silk swinging over the stage. The dancer went into a split high in the air then did a free fall drop, catching herself in the silk. She wrapped her body inside using the silk as a cocoon until she emerged again dangling from the fabric by one leg.

---

[10] Sadly, security is not up to par in many strip clubs. In 1998, a dancer by the name of Claudette was giving a private dance to a customer in the Gentlemen's Club, located in Rochester, New York. Her jealous boyfriend, Bobby Brody, barged into the dance room and shot her in the back of the head, shortly afterward turning the gun on himself. The club is still there. The girls are still dancing, and there is still a lack of security to protect the employees and the clientele.

David decided he'd tip her. Waste some time. Maybe the girl would come and talk to him afterwards. Maybe she knew Lenora. Had to know her. Lenora had always wanted to do a silk show. He wished he could see the girl's face, but it was covered in a white veil. He placed a five on the stage. These dancers never picked up any of the money they were tipped, but merely nodded in acknowledgement. Some guy would come along the stage afterwards and put the money in a bucket. David smiled at the girl as she twirled above him, the lights of the stage almost blinding him. He went back to his chair and waited.

David stared at his watch while his knee bounced up and down. Another half hour passed. Maybe this was all a waste of time. Maybe Lenora left him. Found a rich guy to give her everything she wanted. Maybe he should just leave. Or maybe he should just hang around and catch that bitch in the act, turning tricks, then shoot them both in the fucking head.

"Hello there." A woman stood next to his chair, a veil covering her face.

"Hello back." David wondered why her face was covered. Was she scarred? He didn't think so. Places as fancy as this one don't hire dancers with scarred faces.

"May I?" she asked, motioning to the chair.

"Oh, yeah sure." David guzzled the rest of his beer. "Nice work up there."

"You liked it?"

"Well, yeah. What's not to like?" David shifted in his seat.

"Would you like a drink?"

"No, thank you, but I know what you want." Her voice was calming like the low purr of Mrs. Knibbles, his cat. Under the veil, he saw the same blue shimmer on her skin. Her lips, a striking and violent blue, peeked from beneath the edge of the white lace veil. Strange. None of the other girls were wearing a veil. Maybe she was a feature. David was intrigued, maybe a little excited.

"Uh, hum, you do." He played with his empty bottle. "How much will that cost me?"

The woman placed her hands on David's arms. Her skin was freezing, and it sent shock waves of chilled goose bumps over his skin. "It'll be a bit more than the tip you left, but well worth it."

David looked at the stage. Still no sign of Lenora. *Ah Fuck her. Probably left me anyway.* "Sure. Why not."

Before he knew it, David had handed over his Mastercard and was in the back with the dancer drinking shot after shot of Patrón, sobbing about Lenora and the whole sordid mess of dating a coke addict stripper. The dancer pushed him back against the couch and began dancing for him. She removed everything but the veil. David tried to reach for it, but she kept pushing his hands back. David's head began to whirl, the room spinning and fading in and out of focus. He felt her hand on his zipper, and before he could summon up the willpower to tell her no, she was on him riding him gently into a deeper oblivion.

What was he doing? This wasn't right. He knew this wasn't right. *God only knew what this girl had.* He tried to bring his head out of the drunken fog. This didn't feel right to him. None of it. Her skin was too cold, and even her insides were cold, and yet he couldn't help but explode inside of her. She grabbed his face as her rocking subsided.

"Congratulations," she said as she pulled off the veil. "You were my first."

David mumbled as he tried again to focus. She leaned in and kissed him, biting him on the lips. Blood rose to the broken skin as she sucked on his lower lip. "Ow, hey. Fuck!" David pushed her off him. He stood up bracing the wall as he zipped up. "I gotta get the hell out of here. Hey," he said looking at the dancer, "what the fuck's wrong with you?" Finally, the world had come back into focus. He didn't know if it was the load he blew or the blood she had drawn, but he was happy to have his vision back.

"Why? Did I do something wrong?" She looked at him and David felt the urge to puke.

"Lenora?" He leaned closer. "What the fuck are you doing!" He grabbed her by the arm and wrapped his coat around her. "So, this is how you do it. I knew it." He looked into her eyes and saw no recognition on her end. It was as if all memory of him had vanished. "Hey, it's me. What the hell are you on?" Still nothing in her eyes. No recognition—just a blank, empty stare. Lenora loved her coke, but it never made her like this. There was something wrong with her. "What the hell did they do to you, baby?" He kissed her cheek as tears fell on her blue skin. "I'm getting you out of here." David grabbed the gun from his boot and hurried her to the front of the club towards the door.

Two bouncers quickly stood in front of the door. David pointed his gun at them. "Get out of my way."

"Can't do that, boss."

David pulled the trigger, shooting one of the bouncers in the leg. He fell to the floor like a newborn bird. David aimed the gun at the other bouncer. "Move, or you're next." The bouncer moved to the side as David inched cautiously to the front door, whipping himself around to keep an eye on the crowd.

A tall, well-dressed man approached him. "Stop where you are."

David pointed the gun at him.

"I'm afraid that you cannot take her beyond the threshold," the man said. Lenora reached out for the tall man and began a mournful moan.

David looked at his girlfriend in disbelief and then back to the man. "I don't know what the fuck you did to her, but I'm getting her out of here."

"And just where will you take her?"

"What? To a goddamn hospital!"

"You cannot take her past the threshold."

"Vincent," Lenora moaned as she began to shake.

"Shh, baby," David whispered in her ear. He wanted to shoot this man, this Vincent, this pimp. He kicked open the door with his boot. "Watch me."

David had parked four blocks away. He wanted to stay off the main stretch, so he took his girlfriend through the alleyway. Lenora was shaking worse now than before. She began coughing, and they had to stop as she retched up black fluid as thick as lukewarm tar. He held her hair as he kneeled next to her rubbing her back. "Come on baby. We gotta keep moving. I gotta get you to a hospital."

"Where's Vincent?"

"Forget about that asshole."

"I'm so hungry."

David turned her towards him as he tried to keep the tears from falling from his eyes. "I know. We'll get you some food. Just have to get you check out first." He hugged her. She nuzzled her face into the crook of his neck. He couldn't feel her breath. His heart skipped. Held his breath. "Lenora?"

"I'm hungry now." She bit into his neck, her teeth tearing away a hunk of flesh. Blood spattered the alleyway as David fell back holding his neck. He watched her as she chewed up his flesh and licked his blood from her fingers. Her eyes were a cold, pale-blue and appeared as if the blood vessels had popped, turning the white around the iris a soft pink. She began to crawl towards him when David heard a gun fire. A tranquilizer dart landed in Lenora's neck. Her eyes rolled back as she tumbled to the gravel.

"There you are. I told you not to take her past the threshold." It was Vincent with two of his goons. David tried to stand up, but the loss of blood made it next to impossible. "Get her back before her skin starts rotting off."

Rotting off? She can't be—I had sex with her. She couldn't be. David started puking thinking about her cold skin, their cold sex.

Things happen here that you never thought were possible. It couldn't be. She couldn't be.

"Dead?" Vincent stated looking down at David. "Yes, quite dead and a rare commodity."

David puked again, causing blood to gush harder from the wound on his neck.

"What about him?" One of the bouncers pointed to David.

"Take him in the back. I'm sure the girls are famished by now. We don't need them eating the high rollers." Vincent pulled a cigarette from his pack and lit it. "The show must go on."

TANGIBLE

I can see Chloe crying in her bed. She tries to hide her sobs as she buries her head in her pillows covered in soft cotton. I can't stand the pain coming from her. I watch her body shake against her purple comforter, little green dragonflies embroidered on the edges. She started her period today, and her classmates pointed and laughed at her bloodstained jeans. I only know this because that's what she told her mommy. I could tell that Chloe wasn't consoled properly. Her mommy doesn't know what to whisper in Chloe's ear at night to make the tears stop. Only I know that, and I'm not sharing. Chloe doesn't want to go to school tomorrow. I don't think she should. She should just stay here in this room with me.

She should just hold me again, like she used to. I wish she would hold me again. I remember back when she was eight years old that bastard Jimmy pushed her off the swing. I went flying across the playground, little feet stomping around me. The sun was high in the sky, and I had to keep blinking. I saw my little girl crying, her knees bloodied from her fall. Her mommy and daddy ran to her, but she pushed them off. She was crying out for me. "Where is Zoe!" she kept screaming. Her daddy scooped me up and wiped the small bits of gravel from my blonde hair. I was back in her arms and felt her hot tears on my cold cheeks.

However, now Chloe's tears flow to her pillows. They do not drop to my cold skin. They do not soak my course, blonde curls. I need to go to her. I must be with her. I know she would feel comforted once my cold, stiff body is in her arms again. I need to wait a little more. Wait until she's just about to fall asleep. The last time I went to her, she screamed. She threw me in her closet and covered me with her clothes. It took me weeks to dig through those clothes. I had to wait for her to forget that I was there. Wait for her to let her guard down just enough to leave that closet door open a crack. Then I waited for her to leave for school, for her daddy to go to work, and for her mommy to go to yoga. Once outside of that closet, I needed to figure out how to get on her shelf with those empty, fluffy animals. I grabbed her books and stacked them one by one until it was high enough to reach the shelf, building in little steps along the way. Then I kicked the books over. They made a mess on her floor. The pile of books got Chloe in trouble. I hated seeing her mommy yell at her and not believe her that she didn't throw all her books on the floor, but it was worth it. I hid behind those fluffy animals with just enough of my face showing. Finally, I was able to see her every day.

I watched her for a week. I thought it best if I stalled my return to her arms. Wait for her to forget about the mess I made just to get up here. All this waiting hurts me. I need her heat to enter me. I was prepared to wait longer, but then I saw her crying. Those tears. Those flushed cheeks. The way Chloe's body shook. It needs to be tonight.

As she drifts off to sleep, I push those empty bastards off her shelf. This time I won't leave them on the floor. This time I'll push the evidence under her bed. And I'll find a different hiding place. I push my planning out of my head and jump off the shelf, landing on the fluffy idiots below. I crawl on my hands and knees to her bed. I don't want to walk. My shoes make too much noise. I stand up and pull myself up the side rails. I balance on the wood of the rails and grip her blanket. She shifts as I reach the top. I lie as still as possible until her breath steadies again. I furtively climb to her pillows and pull back the covers. My body is next to her again. I place my head next to hers and look at her face. My eyes blink as her heat touches my skin. I feel my eyelids soften. I am finally able to stretch my mouth from that taut smile. I feel her breath on my skin. My fingers are now warm as I reach out and play with her hair.

THE TEA PARTY

Clarissa turned the invitation over and over, and the delicate paper on which it was printed crinkled with every flip; the silver etched writing glimmered in the peeking sunlight. She couldn't believe that she was back here after so much time had passed. She vowed to never return, but here she was. Sitting in the diner, she stirred her cup of coffee watching the cream swirl in the black liquid until it turned the coffee a uniform light brown. She was never one for tea, always thought it tasted like watered down flowers. Tea: dead leaves served in a cup mixed with honey or delicate sugar cubes. Tea: water pissed through herbs. Most people she knew were coffee drinkers. She peered around the diner, looked at each person's beverage: coffee, coffee, coffee. No tea, no herbal remedies, no lemon, and no honey.

The sun was getting higher in the sky, its warm rays sharper through the slits of the diner's blinds. Clarissa's hangover threw a tantrum. She pulled her sunglasses from the top of her head and slid them over her bloodshot eyes, thankful that the slight shaking of her hands had finally subsided. She tapped the invitation against the table. The invitation that felt so light in her fingertips weighed heavily on her thoughts. As a little girl, she had gone along with Abigail's endless tea parties out of love for her best friend. She would have to do it again, just this last time. She would attend one more tea party, just to ensure that Abigail had picked up the porcelain pieces of her own shattered life.

Blood sisters, now we're bound together forever. They had been eight years old when they made that pact, camping out in a tent set up in Clarissa's backyard as Abigail pulled out her father's straight razor. Wincing and giggling, they pooled their bloody palms in a promised unity. Clarissa looked at Abigail as a friend, but Abigail always wanted so much more.

"More coffee?" The waitress sounded like an automaton.

"No thanks. I should really get going." The invitation slipped out of her hands and reflected the peeking sunlight.

"That's a pretty card," the waitress said.

"It's an invitation." Clarissa pulled out her wallet from her back pocket. She was never one for purses or makeup, dresses or high heels. She oversaw dressing skinny girls in high fashion. That was as close as she cared to get to a pair of stilettos. Clarissa peered at the waitress through her shaggy blonde bangs. "It's a Victorian tea party."

"Sounds charming. You might be a bit under-dressed." The

waitress set her coffee pot down, then pulled Clarissa's check out of her waitress pad.

"Under-dressed. Huh, under-prepared, that's what you mean." Clarissa handed the waitress enough for the bill and a few bucks extra for tip. "Yeah, charming," she said as she grabbed her wallet and slid out of the booth.

A charming tea party to cover up the scars. Frilly napkins and crocheted tablecloths to hide the loss. Bouquets of flowers to adorn a now empty home. Finger sandwiches and bite sized pies to fill the void. Clarissa paused before she opened the door to her car. She looked at the rolling hills that stretched behind the diner, covered in green grass. Nearby she noted the perfect gleam of the white picket fences that sheltered neighbor from neighbor. *Fuck this place, this town, and this shadow of what life is meant to be.* She missed the city already. Missed the noise, the shoving and pushing. Missed the deadlines. Missed the shots of bourbon at the end of the day. Today would be filled with cucumber sandwiches and wide brimmed hats with pastel sashes. "Charming," she sighed and got into her car.

Once they had run together in little white dresses, with little white shoes, watched by doting parents and envious friends. When Abigail had moved into a large Victorian house on the outskirts of town, Clarissa had moved to the city. Abigail planted flowers. Clarissa pasted fashion on skeletal girls. Abigail hosted garden parties, had married rich, and had a daughter. Clarissa slept alone, surrounded by full ashtrays and empty bottles of bourbon. Clarissa turned the volume up on her radio to drown out the past, but as she drove further, the past screamed back at her. She wouldn't even be here if it hadn't been for the accident.

She found the driveway to Abigail's house. The party was at one. It was quarter after. Abigail would be angry. God forbid things didn't happen in an orderly fashion—in Abigail's fashion.

To say the house was in Victorian style would be insufficient. It was painted a deep violet with cream trim. There were spires and arches, a wrap-around porch, and mammoth double oak doors adorned with flowery Tiffany stained-glass windows. "God," Clarissa muttered as she made her way out of her car. The driveway was paved with brilliant red bricks—no gravel stones to dislodge a high heeled foot here—and was devoid of weeds or insects, from what Clarissa could see. The front yard was illustrated with a kaleidoscope of flowers weaving in delicate designs of swirls and circular patterns. Pansies of purple and yellow were protected by cascading stalks of pink gladiolas. Purple heath blossoms were serenaded by white rosemary ledums. Yellow jasmine wrapped around the wooden archway leading to the backyard. Gigantic wisteria blossoms boasting a brilliant violet kissed the sides of the house. Bulbous orange honeysuckle and droopy white rhododendrons carved a path to the purple clematis, whose pale-cream colored centers reached for the sun. A darker violet morning glory, almost star shaped and outlined in white, wrapped around the side of the porch, seeming to choke the wooden structures. Lily of the valley bowed and appeared to cry in a bell-like fashion underneath the boisterous day lilies. Row upon row of little blue forget me nots presented themselves on either side of the walkway that led to the backyard. Purple touched pink kissed white hugged orange caressed violet swallowed yellow followed blue.

"Ugh." Clarissa had forgotten her allergy medication. She dove back into the car and grabbed it, unscrewed the top and swallowed a pill with spit. From the car, she heard click-clack, clickity-clackity, click clack. *Abigail and her damn heels, I bet they're even white.* Clarissa stood up and shut the car door. *Yup, white shoes to match her white dress. Oh, look, a pink sash.*

"You made it. I'm so glad you made it," Abigail said as she stopped in front of Clarissa. Abigail and Clarissa were the same age of thirty-two, but somehow Clarissa felt decades older. Abigail's blonde hair was bouncy and full. Her green eyes still had a sparkle. The only sign that Abigail wasn't quite right was the slight twitch of her left cheek.

"I know I'm late." Clarissa crossed her arms. "Sorry."

"At least you're here." Abigail forced an arm through Clarissa's and led her up the front porch and through the double oak doors. As she walked, Abigail hummed a verse of some silly song over and over. Clarissa wished she would stop humming, wished she'd let go of her damn arm. *Stop humming. My head aches.* She felt like she was trapped in some weird childish TV show.

"Hey, thought there was a party." Clarissa yanked her arm away.

"Not dressed like that."

"Give me a break," Clarissa said. She rubbed her temples and leaned against the wall.

"At least let me fix your hair." Abigail retreated to the

downstairs bathroom and returned with a case of toiletries: hairbrush, pins, makeup, and different shades of lip gloss. Her dress flew in a flurry of taffeta and rose-colored ribbons. She dropped the case to the floor, spilling its contents. Abigail huffed and fell to the floor slumped over like one of her lilies of the valley. Her head was bent to the floor glaring at the spilled makeup. She took in a deep breath and let out an equally sizeable sigh. Her hands scrambled to pick up the beauty secrets she kept from most.

"Abby. Abby, will you just stop?" Already Clarissa was losing her patience. Already she wanted to turn on her heel, walk out the stained glass double doors, head down the red brick driveway, get in her car, and go home.

Abigail paused, holding her rouge in her crocheted gloved hands. "I just want you to be perfect. I mean everything should be perfect." Her hands shook, and her lips quivered under tendrils of bright blonde hair. "Stupid. Stupid. Now you'll just leave again."

Clarissa knelt on the floor next to her and grabbed a tube of lip gloss. "This is a pretty shade. What if I just go with the gloss?"

"Well, that—yes, that would be a nice start."

Clarissa opened the gloss and placed the opening to her lips.

"No, let me, please. You were always so clumsy."

Clarissa caved as she handed the gloss to Abigail. She would put up with the insults. After all, Clarissa felt she deserved it. She should have been there for Abby during the funeral. This tea party was her penance. She would give Abigail a kiss and a hug, then head back to Chicago where everything made sense, her duties done and her friend content for at least another eight months.

It seemed to take an eternity for the gloss to go on, but at last Abigail was finished. She quickly collected the contents of her bag from the floor and paused at the sight of a silver dragonfly hairpin. "Oh, this would be just lovely."

"Abby."

"You're right." Abigail threw the pin back into the bag. "You're right. Look at you. Perfect. I'm just glad you're here." Abigail stood up and walked back to the bathroom. Clarissa could hear the cupboards open and close and Abigail's footfall on the solid oak floor. "Better late than never."

"Abby... I'm sorry I couldn't make it for the funeral." She should have been here. Every night for two weeks straight, Clarissa had received phone call after phone call from Abigail. Abigail never spoke, just soft whimpers and sniffles followed by a hang up. Clarissa should have been there for her, but all she could think about at that time was Amanda and her gorgeous tits and her stunning long legs. Amanda and 18-year Macallan scotch. To be fair, it was an amazing month.

"It's okay. You had deadlines and stuff. I was a big mess anyway." She hooked her arm in the crook of Clarissa's again and walked her outside to the little slate sidewalk that wound around the house through an archway to the backyard.

"Thank you for understanding, but I could have made time."

"Now stop." Abigail paused and swung Clarissa to face her. "I'm fine. I know the busy life you must have. I made it through, and I'm fine now." Abigail's cheeks were flushed and her eyes glossy.

"Ah shit, Abby."

"No, I'm doing much better now, especially now that you're here in my home." Abigail gave Clarissa a hug, pressing her bony ribcage into Clarissa's body. She hugged her so tightly that Clarissa felt the need to wait for another breath. Things had become so awkward between the two of them ever since Clarissa decided to leave for Chicago. Abigail had gone as far as throwing herself at Clarissa.

Abby, you don't want this. You want Paul.

I only wanted Paul because I can't have you.

Clarissa shivered remembering that pathetic event. So many years had passed since then.

Abigail finally released her. She placed her hands on either side of Clarissa's face and pursed her lips. "I'm sorry. It's just that I love you so much. But you already know that, don't you?"

Clarissa's heart sank and her stomach churned as Abigail hooked their arms together once again. Abigail began to hum as they proceeded down the sidewalk to the backyard. Abigail broke her humming. "They're all here, by the way."

"Who?" Clarissa asked.

"Denise, Nina, and Gwynn. I told them you were coming, and they just couldn't wait to see you again. Just think, all of our old friends here again."

All of them were my old friends except for Denise. She was always so much more.

Denise had tormented Clarissa all through high school. Not in the typical way that most teenage girls torture each other. Hers was teasing and flirting. For a while only Denise knew Clarissa's secret, and Clarissa knew hers as well. Denise's parents made it clear: trust fund or girlfriend. Denise chose to be a breeder. Denise and Clarissa had kept their love a secret. What had blossomed in high school continued when Denise's husband was away on business.

"Just like old times," Abigail said. She almost skipped down the remainder of the slate walk, pulling Clarissa along for the ride. She ushered Clarissa into the backyard. The table was already set for tea. Little finger sandwiches, a cupcake tree, even some of their old teddy bears and porcelain dolls were set up. *Some of those were mine. Where did she get all of those? My parents?* "Here she is, all the way from Chicago," Abigail boasted.

Denise sat at the table wearing a flowing white dress with tiny blue flowers along the hem. The breeze lifted them occasionally, giving them the appearance of floating. *She always had great legs.* Clarissa broke herself from staring and instead waved a friendly hello. Nina, the quiet one, and Gwynn, the jokester, were playing a game of charades. Gwynn immediately stopped and waved her arms in the air.

"Oh, thank god you made it. These games aren't the same without you." Gwynn rushed to Clarissa, almost tripping over one of the frog statues along the slate walk. Her pink dress was tight, much tighter than she had worn dresses before, and the neckline plunged deeply, exposing a rising cleavage of silicone.

"Wow," Clarissa chuckled. "Look at you."

"Like them? Courtesy of my ex-husband." Gwynn was always the typical gold digger. Her mother, now five times divorced, honed her expensive tastes.

Nina sauntered over, her lips stretched into a waxy smile. Nina had always been the nervous sort. She looked up to everyone for approval but could never love herself. "Hey. Didn't think you'd make it." Her hug was as stiff as her smile. Clarissa remembered when they were teenagers, thinking that maybe she was just awkward. But no, it was just Nina, always nervous Nina. "So, what should we play now? Blind Man's Bluff? Croquet? Pass the slipper?" Nina asked, her lips again stretched into an awkward grimace.

"How about we let the girl sit and enjoy some tea." Denise stretched back in the chair letting the sun hit the hollow of her neck. "I'm sure she's tired."

Clarissa walked to the table and took a seat next to Denise. Nina, Gwynn, and Abigail followed behind with Abigail taking a seat at the head. Denise reached for Clarissa's hands and lightly stroked her fingers under the table. Clarissa withdrew her hand quickly and looked away. *Not in front of Abigail.* She took a quick peek at Denise's legs. *Maybe later, but not now.*

"Glad you came," Denise said, peering at Clarissa, then turned her attention to the head of the table.

"Me too, but I can't stay long."

Abigail got up and busied herself with handing out sandwiches and pouring tea.

"How long has she been... you know?" Clarissa whispered as she hid her face behind a sandwich.

"Worse?" Denise replied, hiding behind a teacup. "Since the funeral. We're waiting for her parents to get back from vacation. She's never been right since she lost Paul and Betsy." Denise took a sip of her tea and looked towards Abigail. "Sweetie, you have truly outdone yourself this time. This tea is exquisite. Where'd you get it?"

"Ah, that's my little secret. My special brew." Abigail winked. "I forgot the photo album." She looked around the table then slammed the teapot on the table. "Oh darn!"

"Honey, it's okay. We're not going anywhere." Denise took a sip of her tea.

"Yeah." She paused. "You're right." Abigail started to chuckle. "You're right." She peered at everyone around the table. "Everyone's right where they should be." She smoothed her hand over her hair, which was already stiffened into a tight bun. "Excuse me, ladies."

Denise nodded. Nina nibbled on a cucumber that had fallen to her plate. Gwynn took another gulp of tea and looked at the ground. Clarissa smiled, "Hurry back. I can't wait to see the pictures."

Clarissa waited to hear the back door shut and then turned to Denise. "I thought she was seeing someone for the depression."

"Well, she was," Nina piped in. "But that ended badly when her shrink tried to change the schedule."

Gwynn nodded. "Then she threatened her, so the shrink tried to pass her off on someone else. She hasn't been in therapy since."

Gwynn polished off the rest of her tea and poured another cup. "Complete with a restraining order from the shrink. The hospital finally let her go. I swear if it weren't for her parents' money and Paul's life insurance, I don't know how she would have survived."

Clarissa's guilt took an even harder hit. All Abigail wanted was to be a surgeon. She was the best, but now that was all gone. Abigail's skill on the operating table put to rest by the loss of her family and these crazy delusions to hold on to her childhood past.

"Thanks again for coming." Denise placed her hand on Clarissa's leg and squeezed. "All she talks about is you. I swear if I eat another cucumber sandwich, I'll puke." Denise took a sip of her tea and held the china against her cheek. "Or look at that goddamn photo album with all those pictures of us as kids. She sent out an invitation every week waiting for you to show up."

"Again. I'm sorry."

"Hey, I don't blame you. I'd stay away too if I could."

"You could've come with me."

"No, I couldn't; we both know that."

The back door slammed, and silence filled the table. Abigail waltzed in holding the photo album. She quickly took her seat and opened the book, her face instantly creased into a beaming smile. Abigail finally looked up. "Everyone, please have more tea." She passed the teapot down the table making sure everyone's cup was full. Abigail lifted her cup in the air as if she were toasting with champagne. "To Clarissa, who took a day off from dressing skinny models to grace us at our gathering."

There was an uncomfortable pause. Denise held up her teacup. "To Clarissa."

"To Clarissa," the others chimed in.

Abigail opened the book. It was full of old photos: little girls playing teatime with fluffy bears and cute bunnies, big wide-brimmed hats from their mothers and satin sashes. Other pictures showed little girls sitting in rowboats on the pond. Clarissa's eyes felt heavy, and her brow began to sweat. *Drinking hot tea in the summer heat, smart.* Clarissa held her head up with her hands and tried to take a deep breath, but her lungs fell short, plunged heavy. She peered around the table, her vision blurrier than a Wild Turkey night. Her head swam in clouds of pink ribbons and hyacinths, of morning glory and honeysuckle. She heard a teacup drop. Her body slumped as everything faded out.

*   *   *

Clarissa's head ached, and her stomach felt woozy. She lifted her head from her chest and realized that she couldn't feel her legs. She opened her eyelids and saw that she was still in the garden sitting at the table. Her clothes had been changed. She now wore a purple dress, full of frills and a white sash.

"Abby?" Her voice was just a whisper, as if it too had been captured in violet taffeta. She looked to her left and saw Nina and Gwynn just sitting there with perfect little smiles plastered on their faces. Their hands lay still on the table, their hair blowing in the breeze. "Where's Abby?" Clarissa tried to move her arms again, but then realized they were duct taped to the sides of her chair. She tried to scream, but her voice was gone. "Where's Abby?" she asked her friends. Again, Nina and Gwynn merely smiled, looking forward. "What the hell's the matter with you?"

Clarissa blinked and opened her eyes wider. Tiny red droplets were rolling down Nina's and Gwynn's necks. The skin looked off, too pasty for their skin tone. She blinked again then realized with horror—their necks weren't human flesh but rather porcelain, their hands, porcelain. Nina and Gwynn were dead, their heads stitched onto life-size porcelain dolls.

"Abby." Clarissa tried to scream her name, but was left hoarse again. "Abby, what've you done?" Clarissa tried to move her legs but found again that there was no feeling. She wiggled her hands against the dress and inched it up. Her legs: pale, pale porcelain. "Abby," she whimpered as her stomach heaved up tea and diner coffee.

Abigail walked into the yard, her dress soiled in crimson rust. She heaved two heavy life-size porcelain arms on the table. "Hey," she said, wiping her brow with a filthy linen napkin, "you weren't supposed to be awake yet." She walked over to Clarissa and blotted her cheeks with the bloody napkin. "You must be thirsty. More tea?"

"No, I don't want any fucking tea! Abby, what have you done? Where's Denise?"

"Denise?" Abby looked around. "You really weren't supposed to be awake yet. It's not sct up. Not perfect."

"What have you done with her?" Clarissa rocked back and forth in her chair. Abigail rushed and held her down.

"Stop that." Abigail wiped Clarissa's forehead again and leaned on the arms of the chair. "Do you want your legs to pop off?"

Clarissa threw up again. The contents splattered off Abigail and landed on Clarissa's purple dress.

"Now look what you've done. Now I have to find you another dress." Abigail walked behind a tree and came back with a large burlap bag, the bottom of it saturated in blood. "Seeing as you can't wait, here," she said as she pulled Denise's severed head from the bag. Abigail slammed the head on the table. "Satisfied?" Abigail turned her back on her.

Clarissa screamed silence and recoiled from her lover's severed head. She drew in a convulsed breath, and then screamed, again nothing. Her lips moved, but no voice would come out. Clarissa had to look away, look anywhere but at Denise's head, that head she had held against her chest at night, those lips that once kissed her. "Are you going to kill me too?" she whispered.

"Kill you, my blood sister? I would never kill you. We have so much to catch up on. And you weren't properly dressed." Abigail leaned in front of her and took her face within her blood-crusted palms. Clarissa tried to move her head, get away from the blood on Abigail's hands. Abigail jerked Clarissa's face towards her. "I love you. Always have." Abigail looked away towards Denise's head. She turned back to Clarissa and ran her teeth back and forth on her lips. "But I wasn't good enough, not like her." She walked toward the severed head and caressed Denise's matted hair. "I have to agree. She did have great legs. Hey,"—she turned back to Clarissa as if she'd had a brilliant idea—"would you like to keep them? Nothing a quick stitch couldn't fix."

Clarissa outright blubbered; the tears and snot mingling and pooling on her chin trickled to the vomit in the lap of her dress. Abigail wrung her hands, clenched her fists then hit herself on the sides of her head. She took a few deep breaths, then stood there staring at Clarissa. She began to hum.

"Will you stop humming that fucking song!"

"But it was your favorite. Remember?" Abigail put her hands out and began to twirl as she sang, "Ring around the rosy, pocket full of posies, ashes, ashes, they all fall down." Abigail fell to the ground cross-legged, her dress a trailing heap of taffeta. "I taught that to Betsy, but she left me. So did Paul." She stood up and straightened out her skirt. "Don't worry. Now we can all be together forever.

Clarissa began to cry again.

"I'll be right back," Abigail shouted over her shoulder. "I gotta get the rest of the parts. You girls don't stitch yourselves."

ROSE HIPS

Emily Wyatt sat in her rocking chair, attempting to submit to an air of tranquil calm; however, the creaking of the old wooden rocker in its back and forth, forth and back strides, did nothing but unsettle her already excited nerves. She ran her long, bony fingers along the creases of her rose-colored linen slacks. Earlier this morning she stood in front of her closet to choose the outfit most fitting for her reunion. The slacks called her name: *Emily, choose me. Emily, I am perfect.* She had almost forgotten about those petal-colored comforts. Her hand reached towards the pants, fingers lingering on the material as her cheeks ran from a cold chill to a warm flush. John bought her those pants on their last vacation. John before he became a beast in front of their children's eyes. Emily's head swirled at the thought of putting the rosy pants on again, the crease still pristine, the smell of the Alps still stuck in their stitches. Perfect. Perfect to see him again. Maybe the replicas of petals on her legs would bring him back to her, make him remember who they were, how they loved, what they meant to each other. Bring her husband back to dear Emily Wyatt again.

The blouse she chose was of no concern to Emily. John was a leg man really, and at her age, her breasts were nothing but a shriveled memory of her youthful past, but how that past still made her seep into a shameful swoon—even in her golden years, her cheeks blushed at the quiver between her thighs. Nevertheless, she chose a delicate crocheted white top with a linen lining. Her hair, long and white, trickled like floating feathers down to her waist. Emily always pinned it up, much to John's protests. Tonight, she would let her tresses hang loose in cascading rich curls of billowing clouds on roses. Tonight, she would once again give John everything he loved about her. Tonight, she wanted her husband to remember, remember them.

Back and forth. Forth and back. The creak, creak, creak of an old rickety rocker. Emily's hands lingered on her rosy hips. She drew her hands to her thin lips and decided to forsake an old lady's fortress of wood and passive sliding.

She tried not to pace the length of the living room—her hands still sliding back and forth on the rose pants. Instead she stood trying desperately to think of something to occupy her time while she waited. Tea. She would make a pot of tea. Sip it one cup after another until D.D. came back with her John.

Emily set about her routine of making tea—slicing lemons, the ends cut evenly off, seeds removed—and perused the assortment of herbals she had gathered: peach, chamomile (but that made her too sleepy), maybe peppermint to settle her stomach. But then in the back of her cupboard she saw it—a box of rose hips tea. She fumbled for the box, standing on her white-slippered, tippy toes to grasp at its flimsy cardboard edges. Her eyes closed to slits as her fingers grasped the container, a smile illuminating the aged lines of her hollow cheeks. *So wonderful, this tea soon to be on my lips. And with these lips I will kiss him, and he will have no choice but to remember.*

Emily and John had often indulged in rose hips tea when they were reminiscing, when they were in love, when they wished to remember the night they had first made love, much against their parents' wishes. It was so long ago, the world around them absolute chaos—wars about to break, business men leaping to their deaths, but what did it matter to a couple of kids who were madly in love? She closed her eyes for a moment, holding the box of tea to her breast, and began to dance in small circles across the linoleum of her kitchen floor. The way they had danced when their parents were away, the way they stole a secret kiss. Why had their parents married? Knowing how crazy she felt for John, knowing how much John adored her. A cruel, cruel trick. That's what they had done to them. Emily stopped dancing, her hands nearly wringing the box. Tears welled past her eyelids. She breathed deeply, releasing her vice-grip on the box of tea. She wiped the tears from her eyes, walked shakily to the stove, and put on the kettle. She still heard the whispers, the long lamenting of their youthful cries and pleas, the resolution of John's voice in her ear.

Forget them. Forget them all. Let's run away, away from this sham, run away so we can be together. John's hands were at her waist as they both stood in the pantry, away from Emily's mother, out of sight of John's father. *I can't live like this anymore. I can't pretend anymore. Let's just leave. Go where they can't find us. Let's just leave this all behind.* John swung her around, kissing her neck, then her lips. A plate slipped from Emily's hands. Footsteps sounded in the hallway leading to the kitchen...

The tea kettle screamed. Emily broke from memories of her past. She walked towards the stove to abate its flames as she discovered that she had dropped her tea cup on the floor.

"Damn." She sighed, side-stepping the broken flowered porcelain to turn off the gas flame of the stove. She peered at the clock hanging on the kitchen wall. *Where was D.D.? He should be here by now.* Emily retrieved the broom from the pantry to clean up the glass. Each swoosh of the bristles brought her mind back to that night so long ago in the pantry. *Swoosh, swoosh, swoosh.* His hands upon her shoulders. Their parents in the other room. *Swoosh, swoosh, swoosh.* The plate smashing to the floor. Footsteps echoing in the hall. *Come away with me. Come with me, tonight.* Swoosh, swoosh, swoosh. *Clean it up, Emily. Clean it up before they see.*

Emily finished with the mess on the floor and turned her attention once again to making tea. She felt the urge to pace again, so she retired in resolution with her steamy cup to the wooden rocker. Let her dream while she waited on D.D. Let her memories dawdle in the past when she was young, and John was healthy. Let her mind rest on the time when they were happy, before their children had forcibly taken her beloved away.

Emily tried to take care of John. At first it was the little things. He couldn't remember where he put things. He lost track of the discussion. But then things changed. She found him wandering at night, talking as if he were still in 1936, as if he were still trying to get her to run away with him. Emily sobbed those nights, coaxing him back to bed. As the months went on John grew worse. Stuck in the same time. Stuck in the same sentence. Asking the same questions, but when Emily would find him, John would just scream and cry, asking Emily where Emily was. He ceased to recognize her.

When he struck her, the children stepped in. They used to be such lovely children, now turned into ungrateful brats stealing her John away *for his own good.* They never brought him home. Told her the doctors said it was the end for her dear Johnny. She begged them to take her to see him, but they were too busy, had to mind their children, had to go shopping, *Daddy won't recognize you anyway. Just let him go in peace.* And here she was in this big old house with no one to talk to, no one to kiss, and no one to kiss her back. Back and forth and forth and back, day by day, week by week, until months then years had passed her by.

The only one who came to see her anymore was D.D., but she knew why her eldest grandson came by. Sure, he'd entertain her with his crazy stories, let her kiss him on the cheek; sometimes he'd even turn on the radio and dance with her. That's when she really missed John. D.D. looked so much like him. But Emily knew why he visited, with his bulging pupils and sweaty face. A few bills here and there. Whenever she opened up her pocketbook, she swore she could hear D.D.'s breath quiver from across the room. Emily knew she shouldn't give him the money, but she sure loved to dance.

Another hour passed by, and then twenty minutes. Emily had stalled her rocking into a slumbering sleep. Her tea cup emptied of the delicious rose hips lay idle in her lap. Her chin nuzzled her breastbone, as her delicate nose made a small snore in the back of her throat. A light commotion on her porch woke Emily from her dreamful wanderings. She tilted her head gently from side to side and set the teacup on the small glass table next to her.

"D.D.?" She walked to the front door and peered out the stained glass. D.D. stood in front of her with his head down, long black hair blowing in his face. "D.D.?"

Her grandson looked up with puffy red eyes. Emily opened the door, and D.D. brushed past her immediately, throwing his head into the palm of his hand.

"What is it? Is there something wrong with Grandpa?" Emily asked, her hands drawn to the sides of her head.

"Well, I just uh…" D.D. started to cry.

"What happened? D.D., what happened to my Johnny?"

"I just think he's better off where he was, Grandma."

"No, you promised. You promised to bring him to me. Now, where is he?" Emily flew into a furry, pouncing on D.D. with gnarled fists that offered no real threat.

"Stop it. Stop it, Grandma." D.D. lifted his arms against her attack. "I did. I did bring him. He's in the car."

Emily stopped swinging. She seemed frozen in a mural of surprise and disbelief. She brought her hand to rest on D.D.'s shoulder. "I'm so sorry," she said. "I shouldn't have hit you." Emily turned her grandson to face her and lifted his chin, so his eye would rest on her and not the floor. "Why is he still in the car? Could you bring him in now? To me?"

"Grandma, I really think I should take him back."

"Shh, nonsense." Emily attempted to remain calm. She was so close to Johnny now. She just had to convince D.D. to quiet his conscience.

"He shouldn't be here."

"This is his home now, and you brought him all this way. You know how broken hearted I've been since your folks stole him away from me. And besides, I can take care of him just fine." She threw her hands into the air as if to proclaim what a strong ox of a woman she really was. "I may be old, but I still have some kick to me yet."

"But Grandma—"

"Not another word."

"I don't think you should see him like this." D.D. continued to cry. His lips trembled. Emily knew he would need his fix soon. In the end, the heroin would win, but at least she would have her lover back again.

"Shh, now you listen to me. That's my Johnny in the car, and I am going to take care of him. Now you bring him to me."

"Please don't make me do this."

"Do you want the money, or don't you?"

"I don't know anymore."

"What?" Emily pushed herself away from D.D. She wrung her hands and stared at the ceiling as if God was somehow hiding from her in its beams. "I can't believe this."

D.D. looked at her. She saw the pain in his face. It was the pain of a child who had been caught doing something very, very bad. Caught doing something that his parents would have been outraged by. She knew that look. She had that look once. She had that look smacked off her by her mother when she saw Emily in bed with her step-brother.

Emily pulled D.D. by the hand to the couch. She had him sit beside her as she leaned on his shoulder.

"I'm so sorry to make you go behind your parents' back. Besides, you were the only one who ever came to visit me. I would hate for our relationship to change now, after how much you looked after me and I looked after you." Emily petted his hand—traced his young skin with her thin-papered fingers. "Besides you," she continued, "Johnny is all I've ever had. He's all I ever needed, and I need him right now. I don't know how much longer I have left,"

"Grandma, don't say that."

"Well, it's true. I don't know how much longer I have, and please," Emily said as she sat up and took D.D.'s face again in her hands, "please let me just be near him again. Even if it's just for a little bit. Then you can take him back. I swear. I just need him to try to remember. Maybe if he remembers, then he can stay here."

"He's not gonna remember."

"Now, now. How can you know that for sure? How can you know if my Johnny won't remember me?"

"I just do."

"Please D.D. Please," Emily begged, holding D.D.'s face in her hands. He looked down at her wrinkled skin, peered into her eyes hiding behind folded and heavy eyelids. Emily held his gaze there, held his face in the palm of her hands.

"Okay. Okay." D.D. brushed her arms away and stood up.

Emily pushed on either side of her, forcing herself from the couch. "Let me just get my pocketbook."

"No, Grandma. I don't want to do that shit anymore. I can't. I can't live like this anymore. Doin' this shit just to score."

"What will you do?"

"Dunno, rehab or something, but I just—I've never done anything like this before."

"I know you're scared, but you'll see. He'll remember me, and everything will be fine. I won't even tell your parents that you brought him here. 'Cause he will have remembered who I am."

"It won't be like that, Grandma. Ah, hell. I'll just get him, but I'm taking him right back."

D.D. stormed out of the house and slammed the door so hard the stained glass rattled against the oak frame. Emily paced the room faster than she had even dared to walk in years. She kept thinking that she needed to straighten something, that there was something that needed to be cleaned, but everything was in its proper place. She heard the car door open and close. She heard a man grunting and the fumbling at the front door. Emily stood next to the couch, her hands nervously moving over her rose pants.

D.D. entered the living room, with Johnny's frail frame thrown over his shoulder.

"Oh, he must be so tired from the trip. Here, place him on the couch."

D.D. huffed and set his grandfather on the couch. He stood back flinging his arms back and forth, looking anywhere but the couch. Emily beamed. She cautiously approached the couch and scooted next to her husband.

"Johnny? Johnny? It's Emily. Do you remember?" But her husband didn't move. He just lay there with his eyes closed, his lips peaceful almost smiling. "D.D., he's smiling. I think even in his sleep he remembers," she gushed.

D.D. turned from her and faced the front door.

"Johnny, oh I want you to wake up. I want you to see me. I just know that when you see me you'll remember me." Emily gave him a shove, but Johnny still lay still, his eyes closed tight. She tapped his cheek, but again no movement. "Oh, why won't he look at me! Why is he being so stubborn? I just know that if he looked at me he'd remember." She gave her lover another tap on the cheek. "D.D., why won't he look at me?" Her voice sounded weak and desperate like a child who didn't understand why her puppy ran away.

D.D. turned and faced Emily. Tears swallowed his face.

"Because his eyes are glued shut. He died three days ago. I told you, Grandma, but you just don't seem to remember anything anymore."

THE DOLL MAKER

Hazel stood on the overpass and watched the cars speeding on the highway below her. In one arm, she cradled a porcelain doll. With her other hand, she pulled out a flask from her back pocket. She drained the whiskey into her mouth and threw the flask below, watching it bounce off the guardrail and land in the shoulder covered in gravel and litter. Her breath grew rapid. She felt goosebumps on her arms and saw her breath in front of her. It was a hot summer's day, but everything around her was like ice. She placed one leg over the edge of the overpass. She held the porcelain doll under her chin and kissed the blonde locks of hair. She gripped the lacy dress. The air in front of her shifted as if a pot of water was boiling sending steam into the environment. It condensed and seemed to vibrate. A woman appeared to her from the vapor, translucent and floating in front of her. Long blonde hair, beautiful white dress.

"What are you doing, Hazel?"

"I have to end it. It won't stop." Hazel kissed the doll and swung her other leg over the bridge.

"No. It won't stop."

Hazel looked at the woman. "They did this. They did all of this."

"Yes."

"Well, I can't be a part of this. I can't hear them. I can't feel them anymore. I have to make it stop."

"I understand. But before you do, I need you to give me the doll."

"Why?" Hazel began to cry as she clutched the porcelain doll to her chest.

"Because it doesn't belong to you."

Hazel cried, her tears falling to the doll's head. She kissed the head of the doll and held it to her cheek. "I don't want to die alone," she said looking at the woman.

"You won't be alone. I will be with you till the end," the woman replied.

Hazel lifted the doll with shaky arms and handed the porcelain doll to the woman. The woman held the doll to her chest and smiled. "Are you ready?" the woman asked.

"No, but I need it to end."

The woman caressed Hazel's face tenderly. She stroked her hair. Then, she twirled a lock of her hair in her fingers and ripped it out. Hazel cried and shook. The woman kissed her forehead. "What else do you need, Hazel?"

"Pay. I need them to pay for what they did."

"It will be done as instructed," the woman said as she kissed her lips and pushed Hazel over the bridge to the racing cars below.

*　*　*

The Litchworth family breathed a guilty sigh of relief. Hazel's mother bought a pink dress for her dead daughter. Everything Hazel owned was black, and she would be damned if her daughter would be seen in black. Much of Hazel's life was shrouded in darkness, but Mrs. Litchworth would have her daughter remembered as she had dreamed she would be but never was: dressed in pink, hair curled, cheeks rosy—feminine. All the preparation that Mrs. Litchworth made fell on an almost empty gathering. She picked up the phone and called her son, Frederick, one more time. The call was sent to voicemail. Mrs. Litchworth cleared her throat.

"Hi, Freddie. It's Mom. I've left you several messages." She cleared her throat again. "I-I know you must know your sister is dead. We all saw this coming. We—uh, I—did what I could on my own. You left, but I don't blame you for leaving." She sighed and wiped the tears from her eyes. "We owe it to her to say goodbye. The funeral is in two days. Uncle Clarence will be here. I would really appreciate it if you would be here as well." She ended the call and slid to the floor. Mrs. Litchworth cradled her head in her hands and sobbed. *Please don't let it just be her and Clarence. Please let Freddie show up. If only Hank were still here. If only Hank were still alive.* Mrs. Litchworth's thoughts engulfed her. She was startled from her despondency when her cell phone fell from the counter. She picked it up to see a spider web break across its screen.

Clarence arrived on time to the minute. He could have flown, but insisted that the drive would help clear his head. Clarence was always there for his sister. He opened his arms and enfolded her in a hug. She wanted to recoil yet didn't. A sense of family guilt overwhelmed her. He was here for her, here when no one else was. "I'm so sorry, Hanna." It was strange for Mrs. Litchworth to hear her first name. She had grown accustomed to hearing mom and Mrs. Litchworth. She almost forgot that she was Hanna. Just upon hearing her name, the word *Hanna,* she began to sob. Clarence held her there standing in the driveway. He kissed her cheek. "Let's get inside," he said as the next-door neighbor stood on her porch gawking at them.

Hanna fed Clarence her famous pot roast that had simmered all day in her crock pot. It was her children's favorite, Hank's too. Her family, dwindled to nothing. There was only her brother, Clarence, here now to join her in supper. Clarence who brought a suitcase of clothes and a suitcase of doll parts. Clarence who would fashion a doll for the departed Hazel, as was his nature to do.

Clarence started his doll-making when he was fourteen. There had been a terrible accident—a young girl fell off a cliff, her poor body smashed beyond recognition on the rocks below. Her frail frame mangled and bruised, bones ripped through flesh, teeth smashed out. Amanda. Hanna once again allowed the poor girl's name to enter her thoughts as Hanna and Clarence sat there in silence at her empty dining room table eating her pot roast.

Amanda. She had been such a happy and carefree little girl. Most of all, Amanda was Clarence's only friend.

Clarence was always a quiet child, reclusive—some would say anti-social. He was always in his room drawing pictures. First it was still-life drawings—flowers, bowls of fruit, his hand—but then entered Amanda. She drew him out of the house and into the outdoors. Then, Clarence drew Amanda: Amanda on the tire swing, Amanda in the garden, Amanda in the crook of their willow tree. Clarence then signed up for pottery classes. He fashioned faces of Amanda from the drawings he saved. When Amanda died, Clarence withdrew in his room once again. He researched doll making and fashioned a doll in her likeness. Clarence attended the funeral. Hanna was with him. He didn't want to go alone, and he needed the strength of his older sister. The adults dwarfed little, lank Clarence as he approached Amanda's parent with his show box. His voice cracked and wavered as he handed the box to Amanda's mother, her eyes so swollen and red, her blue pupils almost appeared purple.

"What's this?" Amanda's mother had asked, crinkling her nose.

"I made it for you, so you could remember her as I do." Clarence stood in front of her and looked to the shiny wooden floor of the funeral parlor. Amanda's mother opened the box. A stifled yelp fled her lips as she looked at a miniature of her daughter. "You made this?" Clarence attempted to leave, but Amanda's mother grabbed his wrist before he could flee. "Why would you do this?"

"I'm sorry. You don't like her. I'm sorry." Clarence wet himself. He ripped his sleeve away from Amanda's mother. He ran from the funeral parlor in tears. Hanna was still standing there.

"He just wanted to do something nice for you and for Amanda," Hanna said as she watched her brother barrel out the door.

Amanda's mother took the doll out of the box. She began to sob as she kissed the porcelain cheeks of the doll. "She's beautiful. She's Amanda, but it's inappropriate." She placed the doll back in the cardboard box. "You know why. Your brother should have known why, probably did know, but that didn't stop him, did it? She is beautiful." Amanda's mother caressed the cheek of the doll. "He certainly has an eye. Captures beauty, doesn't he?"

Hanna blushed.

"Tell your brother I said thank you." Amanda's mother closed the box and looked forward. Hanna was no longer needed in her reality.

As much as Amanda's mother was upset, word spread. Clarence had a gift. Lost a daughter? Lost a son? Clarence could make you a doll. Between homework and chores, Clarence busied himself with death dolls for bereaved parents. Because there were plenty of children to grieve. Not from sicknesses. Not from accidents. A predator was in their midst.

The cops finally captured him, Thomas James. There were trinkets in his trailer home: necklaces, ball cards, even homework assignments. Thomas James was sentenced to death and executed. His trinkets after a fashion were returned to the grieving parents. Clarence was also there with his dolls. The children were all marred beyond recognition. Their faces had been removed. Thank god for

Clarence. That killer took their children's faces, took their personal belongings, but thank god for Clarence. He gave the bereaved what the killer took. The bereaved sought him out, gave Clarence pictures of their young departed. Clarence would work tirelessly to replicate their babies into a perfect porcelain doll. Of course, Clarence always made two dolls. His business had become lucrative, and he needed his work as a testament.

"I see you brought your other suitcase." Hanna wiped her mouth throwing the linen napkin in her empty bowl.

"Yes, of course."

"I don't want you making my Hazel into a doll." Hanna looked off to wipe away a tear as if looking to her right side would make that moment disappear.

Clarence smoothed the remnants of the roast from his spoon into the small of his tongue. He set the spoon neatly to the right of his bowl. He wiped both sides of his mouth with his linen towel. He folded the towel into even thirds upon itself, then set the towel to the left of his bowl. He placed his hands on his legs and smoothed down his pants. He looked at his sister. "Why else would I be here?" He steepled his hands beneath his chin. His pinky fingers smoothed out his mustache. "Why else would you ask me to be here?"

"I asked you here to remember your niece, my daughter." She stared forward, avoiding Clarence's entreating gaze—his look for her approval of a new doll.

"And I will remember her. We both will remember her."

"There should be more here to remember her." Hanna stood up and grabbed the empty dishes from her mammoth dining room table. She stopped and turned to Clarence as she cradled the dirty dishes against her breasts. "But we won't be remembering her, not my Hazel, like that."

Clarence looked at his legs. He sighed.

"Promise me you won't do that to her, Clarence. Don't make her into one of those *things*."

"I," Clarence started as he began to rub the legs of his pants. "I already have."

Hanna sighed. "Just don't show it to me." Hanna set the dishes down. She placed her hand under his chin and guided his head upwards, so he would be forced to look at her. "I mean it. I don't want to see it. I can't see it. Please."

Clarence sighed. Hanna let go of his jaw and picked up the dishes. She walked into the kitchen. Clarence followed.

"I already made her, and she is perfect. Just see her. Just see how perfect I made her."

Hanna threw the dishes into the sink. The plates crashed and broke against the copper sink. Hanna turned. "I made her! She was perfect from me! She's not another one of your dolls!" Hanna slumped to the floor.

Clarence knelt in front of her. His eyes darted back and forth for a moment then focused on Hanna's eyes. He held his sister's face in his hands and wiped away her tears. "I just wanted to make her perfect, perfect for you."

"I can't. I can't. I won't." Hanna attempted to get up. Clarence pulled her hands down, keeping Hanna pinned to the cold tiles of her kitchen floor. Hanna attempted to disentangle herself from Clarence's grasp. He held her, as she struggled against him.

"I made her for you."

"And yourself. Just as you did Amanda. That was wrong. And you know it. This is all wrong. Has been wrong."

"May Girl."

"Amanda. Her name was Amanda, not May Girl. She was our sister. This is my daughter. I won't have you do this to my daughter. Not that. Not what you did to Amanda. My daughter will not be another one of your dolls. Not like our sister." Hanna held her hands up. Clarence still grasped them. "It was wrong. I should have kept after you better. Should have kept you from that girl."

Clarence pulled Hanna's hands to his cheeks and held them there. He kissed her forehead. He kissed her cheeks. His lips touched her ears. "I love you. I love you. I love you. I love you." He smoothed Hanna's hair away from her sweaty forehead. "I forgive you."

"Forgive me?" Hanna wished Clarence wasn't here. She wished secretly that he was the one who fell off the cliff. She wished that her half-sister Amanda had lived, and that Clarence was smashed to bits.

"Yes, I forgive you. I forgive you for bringing up May Girl." He began to stand and drew Hanna to her feet as well. "You just need to rest. When you're ready. When you're ready I'll give you Hazel."

Clarence looked at the smashed dishes in the sink. "I'll clean this up. It will help me. It will." He kissed her, this time on the lips. Hanna knew better than to withdraw from Clarence. Her gut wrenched but externally she remained soft. "This will help from me being angry about May Girl."

Hanna locked the bathroom door before she turned on the shower. Normally the doors in her house were never locked, but childhood habits returned full force with Clarence below in her kitchen. Although he never implicitly violated her, she felt an indecency in him. Although he never touched her, his kisses lingered too long for a brother, the way he looked at her, the fact that he found reasons to walk in on her when she was changing. What he did with Amanda, his May Girl, that she could never erase from her memory.

The hot water pouring over her head did not ease Hanna's nerves or her aching pain that left her feeling empty and without purpose. She had seen his pictures. The secret ones. The ones Clarence had hidden under his comic books. Clarence was too smart to hide those pictures in an underwear drawer or under his mattress. Those places would be the first place a mother would look for contraband of any sort. But comic books? What would a mother want with comic books? Hanna knew Clarence. She knew that his new friend was not a friend. She was dirty. She was loose. She was their father's dark secret. An affair. She was their sister. Clarence didn't know about it. Hanna only knew about it because she was a sneaky bandit, ever quiet, holding her breath when the adults would speak, when the adults would argue in hushed whispers regarding the mistakes of their past, thinking that all the children were asleep. Hanna was not asleep.

She had seen the pictures that Clarence drew, the pictures of Amanda naked. She found them together. Their parents weren't home. Hanna in her silent manner walked into the house. She sat in her room for a bit listening to her Walkman. After the third song, Hanna's stomach began to grumble. She decided to make a peanut butter and jelly sandwich. She also decided to stop by Clarence's room and see if he was hungry too. Clarence would get so wrapped up in his art that oftentimes, Hanna had to remind him to eat. Hanna still had her Walkman blasting in her ears. She didn't hear the panting coming from Clarence's room. She rapped on the door and just entered. She wasn't even looking when she first entered.

"Clarence, do you want a peanut butter and jelly sandwich?" Hanna said louder than she needed to due to the blasting music. She finally looked at his desk, but Clarence was not there. She looked to the bed and saw Clarence and Amanda in shock, scurrying for their clothes. Hanna's jaw dropped as she witnessed their naked bodies trying to find cover. Amanda pulled up her underwear and grabbed her dress hurriedly pulling it over her head. Clarence struggled to find his jeans. Amanda pushed past Hanna and dislodged Hanna's Walkman from her hands. It smashed against the floor, ripping the headphones from her head.

"Clarence, oh my God. Clarence."

"Get out!" His face flushed red.

"Clarence, you shouldn't have. Oh my God."

"Get the hell out!"

Hanna walked blankly to the kitchen and made two sandwiches. She sat at the kitchen table and waited for Clarence to come out of his room. Thirty minutes went by before his bedroom door finally opened. Clarence sheepishly walked to the table, sat down, and started eating his sandwich. Hanna took a bite of her sandwich.

"I'm not gonna tell Mom and Dad."

"I don't want to talk about it."

"We need to talk about it."

Clarence swallowed another bite of his sandwich and gulped down half his milk. "So, what. So, you saw me having sex. What? A freak like me can't have sex?"

"You're not a freak."

"Really? Everyone at school thinks so except for you and May Girl. She loves me, and I love her."

"You can't love her, not like that."

"Why? You believe what they say about her too? Well she's not like that. She's not a slut."

"She's our sister."

At Hanna's words, Clarence's hands began to shake. "You're a liar."

"It's true. I heard Mom and Dad talking about it. When Amanda and her mother moved here, I heard Mom and Dad talking about it. Dad cheated on Mom. Amanda is your sister."

"You lie. Why wouldn't they tell us? You just don't want me to be happy. Maybe you see me as a freak too."

"Clarence, I'm not lying. I don't know why they wouldn't tell us. Maybe our sister wasn't supposed to come back here. You can't do that again. You need to stay away from her." Hanna stood up and cleared their dishes from the table. Clarence followed her into the kitchen. Hanna placed the dishes in the sink. When she turned around Clarence was in front of her. He placed his hands on the counter, one on each side of Hanna. His face was so close to hers.

"I see what's going on. You're jealous. That's why you're making all this up."

"I'm not making it up." Hanna was getting nervous. Clarence had always been so docile and quiet.

"You're jealous. You know you are," he whispered in her ear. "Jealous that no one has touched you. Jealous that your freak brother got some before you did." Clarence placed his lips on her cheek. "Maybe you're a bigger freak than I am."

Hanna shoved Clarence's chest, but he wouldn't move. "Is that it? Jealous that I didn't draw your picture anymore? Jealous that I fell in love and that she loves me?" He continued to whisper. "If you weren't my sister, I would have fucked you too."

"You're sick."

Clarence kissed Hanna on the lips. She tried to move her head. Clarence grabbed her chin keeping her pinned as he continued to kiss her. "No, Hanna, you're sick." Clarence let go of her and stepped back. "I'm going back to my room." He looked her over. "You might want to clean yourself up. Mom and Dad will be back soon." Clarence walked away from her and slammed his bedroom door. Hanna looked down and realized she had pissed herself.

Hanna's body released those memories as urine ran down her leg mingled with the water from the shower and drizzled down the drain. She sobbed louder unaware that Clarence could hear her. Unaware that Clarence was smiling as he washed their dinner dishes.

Fragmented. Hanna wished she could compartmentalize. She wished she could put Clarence in a box in her mind and only let him out when necessary. She supposed that now was one of those times, but Hanna did not want to let him out of his box with only her to keep him in place. She wished she had a box for her daughter. Not the box Hazel would be burned in. Not the urn that her ashes would rest in. Hanna wished she had a strong glass box that she could have placed her daughter in—a box that only Hanna would have the key to, a box that only she could see into, a box that would have kept her safe from the monsters who drove her to her death. Most of all, Hanna wished she had an iron-clad box to put that damn May Girl in—a box completed with strong nails, no hinges, no. She would have nailed that box shut so that girl would have never come out. May Girl—no just say her name—Amanda, would have never crossed Clarence's path. He would have remained innocent, at least that is what Hanna thought. She would have grabbed her illegitimate sister, perhaps one day on her walk home from school, grabbed her and tossed her in that iron box and nailed the lid shut with her screaming inside. Clarence had reached Amanda first. Sent her flying from the cliff. No lid to keep her screams stifled. Her screams echoed up the jagged rocks and filled the air. Her screams always free to return and torment them once again.

For now, Hanna would construct that cold, glass box for her daughter. She remembered Hazel as a child, remembered her constantly skinned knees from trying to jump double-dutch. She remembered how much Hazel hated the dresses Hanna made her wear. She took her and placed her daughter in that glass coffin. She kissed her cold, still cheeks and shut the lid. Hanna turned off the light on her night stand and shut her eyes. With her eyelids closed, the glass coffin lid lifted. Hazel lifted herself out of it, not dressed in the peach dress Hanna picked out for her, but instead clad in the outfit she was found in. Baggy jeans and a flannel shirt. Hazel wore what would hide her figure. She crawled out of the coffin. Her arms were bleeding. She wiped a bloody wrist across her face as her ghost tears streamed down her cheeks.

Hanna opened her eyes attempting to will the image of her daughter away. Hazel stood at the foot of her bed and continued to wipe her bloody arms across her face. Hanna reached over and turned on her light. She remained, her Hazel, standing at the foot of her bed. Hanna closed her eyes. She felt two hands grab her feet, felt Hazel's fingers touch her through the blankets. Those hands crept up and took hold of her ankles. Coldness seeped from those fingertips into Hanna's skin, her flesh, her bones. Hanna felt her body pulled down the bed. The glass coffin cracked. Hazel was out. There was nothing to keep back the screaming. Hanna wailed and screamed as May Girl must have screamed flying over the cliff.

Clarence rushed up the stairs and threw his body against Hanna's locked door. Hazel opened her mouth. There was no tongue, no teeth, just a huge gaping hole. Blood flowed from her mouth onto Hanna's Queen Anne's Lace comforter.

Clarence assumed Hanna just had another nightmare. He found her at the end of her bed entangled in her sheets and blankets. She was screaming and writhing and saturated in sweat. At first, she pushed at him as he attempted to control her flailing arms and legs.

"Shh, shh, shh, easy there," Clarence whispered against her clammy cheek. "It's just a dream." Hanna continued to push. "It's not real. Just come back to me."

"Get off me. Get off." Hanna pushed against his arms as Clarence attempted to still her. She thrashed for a few more moments before succumbing to his embrace. He listened to her hurried breath and breathed slowly against her cheek. Eventually Hanna's squirming quieted and her breath eased itself to a slow, steady pace.

"Just a dream," Clarence said. "Just a terrible, terrible dream."

The day of the funeral was not a typical funeral type of day. There was not a cloud in the sky. No rain to fall on the pavement. None of that mattered. Barely anyone showed. Hanna couldn't blame the town. Clarence was here, and his presence brought back the memories of the young dead. Hanna had scoured Hazel's apartment, asked the police to assist her in unlocking Hazel's phone just so she could call Hazel's friends and ask them to be at the funeral. Most of the calls she made went to voicemail. A couple people hung up on her. Hanna sat down in the front pew. Clarence sat beside her. Two members from her church showed up. Their appearance was self-serving. They would go back to their friends and gossip about Hanna's pathetic funeral for her departed daughter. Hanna could feel them staring at the back of her head. There was one person who didn't quite fit in. It was a woman as young as Hazel. She wasn't dressed in black like the few who had attended, but rather in a white frilly dress that one might see at a tea party.

Hanna had to give the eulogy herself. There was no one else to do it. Clarence had offered, but Hanna would not hear of it. The town's doll maker had come back. His dolls once brought a sense of closure for the families who had lost their children, but as those cases of the dead built up there was suspicion and hatred focused around the craft of the doll maker. Hanna doubted that the town folk even remembered her brother's name. Hanna tried to stop thinking about Clarence and all those dead kids, ten in total spanning over three years. Someone was arrested for the murders, some dirty drifter; but Hanna didn't believe he did it. The town didn't buy it either. Hanna kept quiet about her suspicions yet was outspoken when Clarence received an odd look or brusque reaction. She breathed a sigh of relief when Clarence decided to attend college out of state, across the country. Their parents wanted Clarence to stay close, but Hanna and Clarence knew it was for the best. When Clarence left, Hanna was finally free to be herself. She no longer locked the bathroom door. She no longer locked her bedroom door. It did take her a couple of months to feel that she was finally free of him, to feel free to leave herself unprotected by an unlocked door. There were times she had to remind herself that she didn't need to lock that door. Then the deaths started again, this time with babies: SIDS, leukemia, a handful from AIDS. One by one the desperate parents approached her. "Please, call Clarence. Please, we just want to remember." Taxidermy via porcelain. Now Clarence had made a doll of her Hazel. She didn't want porcelain. She didn't want a thing. She wanted her daughter back, but not in the way she appeared last night. Clarence kept telling her it was a nightmare, but don't you have to be asleep to have a nightmare?

The woman in the white dress sat in the pew until the few people who attended left. It was then that she stood and approached Hanna. Clarence was next to his sister, his arm draped over her shoulder. Clarence looked at the woman and took in a breath. The breath agitated the hairs on the back of Hanna's neck.

"Mrs. Litchworth, may I speak with you?"

"Yes, of course. Are, I mean, were you a friend of Hazel's?"

"I am." The woman looked at Clarence then back at Hanna. "Can we talk alone?"

Hanna kissed Clarence on the cheek and asked him to give them some space. Clarence protested, but finally agreed to walk away all the while looking over his shoulder to glance at the two women. Hanna and the woman in white sat in the front pew of the church.

"Tell me, how did you know my Hazel?"

"That's not why I am here. I received something from Hazel on the day she died. A letter with instructions."

"A letter? Why didn't you find me before now?"

"It wasn't in the instructions. I was to find you on the day of Hazel's funeral." The woman reached in her purse and pulled out a key. "She wanted me to give you this." The woman placed the key in Hanna's hand. "Uncle Dan's on West Elm Road."

"The storage facility?"

"Yes, the unit number is on the key." The woman stood up. Hanna stood up as well.

"What's in there."

"I'm only following instructions." The woman began to leave the church.

But, wait!" Hanna began to sweat around the collar of her dress. This woman, this stranger was leaving her. This woman had answers. She may have been the last person to see her daughter alive. "What's your name?"

"That wasn't part of the instructions."

Hanna sat in her tub. The bubbles should have been high and thick, kissing her chin, but they all fizzled like weak dead fruit flies caught on dirty dishes sitting in rancid water. Instead of her loofah, Hanna held the key to the storage facility. Hanna wanted to leave the fizzled bubbles of her tub and just go to bed, but she had this key. She should be there right now, unlocking the door to see what was kept inside. Hanna instead chose to take the glass of Sandman port and pour the remnants down her throat. It burned her empty stomach but filled her taste buds with a thick sweet lingering hold.

Hanna heard a noise. A soft gurgle. A slurp of water filing down slits of metal, echoing in the porcelain. Hanna looked about her. She heard it again. A gurgle. A murmur. Metal, and water, and porcelain, and air, till it slurped again.

Familial bonds, family trying to hold a concept of family. What is the concept? She placed the key atop the side of the tub. The flaccid bubbles began to percolate, intensifying in the heat of the water. Hanna drew herself up as the bubbles enlarged and popped. The bubbles were an ivory sheen towering above the faucet of the tub. Hanna felt a pang in her stomach reaching her anus. Saliva collected underneath Hanna's tongue. Her flesh puckered, covering her in gooseflesh. Her stomach panged again making Hanna feel as if she would shit herself right there in the tub. The water between her legs stirred. Two hands broke through the bubbles. Arms reached out, and the hands of a woman gripped the sides of the tub. Hanna wanted to run from the tub, but she filled with fear, felt pinned to the porcelain sides of the tub. A woman began to rise. She was naked except for the bubbles that scattered over her body. Her long hair matted against her face as she looked up. Hanna recognized her daughter.

"What do you want?" Hanna shouted.

Hazel opened her mouth to speak, but lacking a tongue, was unable to.

"What do you want?" Hanna shouted again.

Hazel moaned pointing to the key on the floor. Hazel could hear Clarence's footfall on the steps. The door knob turned, but

Hanna had locked the door. "Hanna? Hanna? Open the door."

Hazel looked at the door and began to shake. She turned to her mother and pointed at the key, then disappeared. Clarence pounded on the door frantically trying to get in.

"I'm fine. Please, just go away."

"You didn't sound fine."

"Just go away." Hanna waited to hear Clarence walk back down the stairs. She pulled out the drain plug, grabbed her towel, and picked up the key from the bathroom floor.

Hanna took in a sharp breath when she turned on the light to the storage unit. There had to be at least fifty porcelain dolls strewn across the concrete floor. There were little girl dolls. Little boy dolls. One thing was clear to Hanna: they were all replicas of children. Some of the dolls she recognized as the young dead from her town. Most of them she had never seen before. The light flickered, and the already chilled air became colder. A box flipped over, and four dolls tumbled to the floor. Hanna stared at the dolls as her daughter Hazel appeared once again. Hazel lifted her foot and stomped on the head of one of the dolls. Hazel pointed to the smashed porcelain face and moaned. Hanna walked to the destroyed doll head and knelt on the floor beside it. She ran her fingers through the destroyed doll head and retrieved a lock of blonde hair. Upon holding that lock of hair in her trembling fingers, Hanna felt light headed. The room was spinning and faded into darkness.

Hanna felt as if she were in a dream, but knew the images flashing before her did not come from her imagination. She saw

Clarence standing in an abandoned alleyway. A girl of about eight years old cried as he approached her. She sobbed for her mother. She begged to go home. Hanna saw Clarence push the girl to the pavement and wrap his hands around her little throat. He choked her until the girl's eyes rolled back. He didn't stop until the girl was dead. He smoothed her hair away from her face, kissed her forehead, got up and left her dead body in the cold, dark alley.

The image of the alley disappeared as a new scene took over. It was Hazel's apartment. Boxes were being delivered. Hazel was on the phone arguing. "But I don't want them," she said as another box was brought in her apartment. "Because they're creepy." She signed the paperwork as the final box was set down. Don't worry. I won't open any more boxes. If anything, I'll put them in storage."

But she continued to open the boxes. The curiosity was too strong not to. She looked at the dolls, and that is when Hazel's nightmares began. Hanna watched as her daughter tossed and turned in sweat-filled sheets. Hanna looked on in horror as phantoms of children appeared around her daughter's bed. Hanna was horrified as Hazel awoke screaming while little hands clawed at her.

She saw her daughter move the boxes to the very storage unit Hanna was in. But the hauntings did not cease for Hazel. Rather they became much worse. Hazel couldn't eat. She was not allowed to sleep. She stopped going to work. She stopped talking to her friends. Hazel was beyond unraveled, and one evening she opened a bottle of whiskey and started drinking. Hazel called a cab and was dropped off at the storage unit.

"I call upon Margaret. They told me to call on you. How do I make them go away?" Hazel whimpered in the night air.

The images faded, and Hanna's sight was restored. She pulled herself from the floor. She heard footsteps behind her and turned to see Clarence picking up one of the porcelain dolls.

"She was only supposed to have them for a few weeks. I told her not to open the boxes. Hazel was always a curious child."

"All these dolls. All those children." Hanna lifted a lock of hair. "You killed them. You killed all those children. And Amanda, your May Girl, you killed her too, didn't you?"

"It was an accident."

"Was it?"

"Of course, it was." Clarence approached Hanna.

"You stay away from me." Hanna backed away. Hazel was standing next to Clarence, who was smiling as she looked at him. "These dolls, those children, it drove my daughter to her death." Hanna looked around the room and saw the spirits of the dead children one by one rise from the porcelain dolls. "I should have said something. I knew. I knew all along. I should have told someone."

"And yet you didn't," a woman's voice rang out. Hanna and Clarence turned to the opening of the storage unit and saw the woman in the white dress. "You kept silent. Their deaths are as much your fault as they are his." The woman began to shift, becoming smaller, becoming younger.

"May Girl," Clarence whispered.

"Don't speak to me." The woman pulled a doll from behind her back. She set it on the floor in front of Clarence. She turned to Hanna. "Your daughter called to me the night she killed herself. The killing stops now. The silence and the lies stop tonight." She walked to Hanna and kissed her forehead. She placed a lock of hair in her hands.

The light flickered and turned off. The only light was from the street lamp illuminating around the form of Amanda Margaret. Hanna watched in horror as she slid the door of the storage unit shut. Hanna pushed Clarence out of the way as she rushed to the door and banged against the cold metal. Hanna heard Clarence cry out. She heard the ripping of clothes and skin. She felt little hands claw at her dress and dig into her flesh. Hanna slammed her hands and head against the door.

"Open the door! Open the goddamn door!"

Amanda Margaret chuckled on the other side. "That wasn't part of the instructions."

CHORES

November 18th

Dear Diary,

I have to write this out, keep a log so to speak. If I do, then maybe it will all make sense. There is so much to do: dishes, laundry, rake the leaves, and dust the furniture. I know I am forgetting something. I always forget something, and he's always there right behind me to remind me of my blunders. I'm a mess, a rotten housewife. I don't deserve him. That's what all his friends tell me. Not so much with their words but with their waning smiles and half-ass gestures of accepting me into their circle. I am beneath the family name. That's what his family tells me. Again with disapproving glances. The house is never clean enough. My attire is too modern for his mother. My education too lacking to appease his father who is still upset that his son didn't settle with a nice Baylor girl. After all, his father has a nice Baylor girl, and she has proven through the decades to be a competent wife.

I met Jack in a bar, one of those local taverns where people sit quietly before a big screen TV, staring at the images while drowning their problems with viscous liquor. I had lost another job in a long list of jobs at places where I didn't quite fit in. My waistline too slender, my skin too unblemished, my hair too thick and long. I never bragged about my looks. I think I saw it more as a curse than anything. Always getting picked on by the girls growing up, boys always trying to trick me out of my pants—no one ever took me seriously. So why should I?

I remember raising my hand to the bartender for another shot of tequila. That's when I met him. Jack. At first, I saw him as just another man who wanted to get his dick wet, but two months later, much to his parents' dismay, we got married. I really don't know why I did it. Maybe I was tired of the constant game, the constant struggle to pay the bills, the constant attempt at a life. Maybe that's why I am still here. Jack has a great job and a beautiful home. What did I have back then? A tiny apartment and bills that I couldn't afford to make a dent in. Look at me now. I am the woman in his life—the one who hangs his shirts neatly in a row: three-quarters of an inch apart, lights to dark, all arranged by appropriate color, in appropriate season.

What's wrong with me? I should be ecstatic. I should be happy. I should be grateful that Jack ever gave me a second look.

Dishes, laundry, dust the furniture, rake the leaves. There is something else. Something important that I should be doing, but I just can't think of it. God, I'm so stupid sometimes, always forgetting the most important thing. Every day it seems I struggle with this. My stupid, stupid brain. Maybe Jack's parents are right. He should have married someone better, a Baylor girl, a girl with a degree, a girl with a fucking brain, a girl who remembers what needs to be done. Laundry, rake the leaves, dishes, dinner? Maybe that is it. Maybe it's dinner. So much to do. So much to do.

November 17th

Dear Diary,

One day I will look back through this diary at the words I wrote and then it will all make sense. Maybe by writing this all down I can be better. I am so angry at myself. How my mind seems foreign to me. How I can't keep things straight. The failure of it all. It wasn't dinner! I went through all that trouble of setting up for a dinner party that wasn't until Friday! The 19th not the 16th! So much food wasted. Jack was pissed. It isn't that we can't afford it, but he watches every dime I spend, often going through my purse to gather all my receipts for the day. I've been so tired lately, what with everything that needs to be done. I broke down and bought a Red Bull earlier today. Jack was so pissed when he found out. He doesn't condone me spending almost three bucks on an energy drink when we have coffee and travel mugs at home. I thought that I had thrown away the receipt, but there it was, my guilty crime hidden in a side pocket of my purse. He would have found out about it anyways. I just didn't want to deal with his anger today. He stood in front of me at the kitchen counter waving the receipt from the gas station in my face.

He scolded me for spending money on a Red Bull. I didn't want to look at him. I knew what I would see. Sure enough, his face was becoming red, the vein in the middle of his forehead enlarged, pulsing. That damn vein always throbbed when he was agitated with me. I had to think of something to say, some excuse no matter how futile.

I tried to apologize to explain my actions. I was tired with all of the errands and the upkeep of this giant house. He just scoffed at me, stating that he worked every day. How he didn't throw away money on frivolous drinks. One thing that I will never forget is what he said to me before he went upstairs to watch his football game, He slammed the receipt on the counter making me jump, and then he said without even looking at me but rather above me as if I was too low of a person to acknowledge: How did you ever survive?

If only he would let me work. I begged him to at least let me waitress again. Absolute no. No wife of his would be slinging food. That was my last chance at independence. At least as a waitress, I would have some cash tips that he wouldn't be able to keep track of. My mind wandered away from my freedom to the task at hand. I had to make him happy. I had to keep on track: clean the gutters, mop the floors, vacuum, and something else. There was always something else. There always was. I heard the game blaring as I tried to recall what chore I had forgotten. I write in this damn diary every day. Why don't I make a to-do list? But, no. Only a dense woman would need a to-do list. His Baylor mother never needed a list. I would be a laughing stock again. If he could find my receipts, he would find my list. I keep this diary down in the basement hidden behind the bleach. Jack never comes down here. Laundry is my job. See, my mind is wandering already.

After he stormed off, I stood at the counter staring at the receipt for my Red Bull. How did we get to this place? How did I get to this place? A woman left devastated over a three-dollar energy drink. I felt the tears begin to well up in my eyes. I felt the knot in my throat and the snot build in my nose. Get yourself together. Get yourself together. That's what I tried to tell myself. I was hoping that repeating that sentence in my head would keep the tears from flowing, would get the knot in my throat to subside. I could hear the grunts and the crash of helmets from his surround sound upstairs. I could picture him up there, sprawled on the couch, surrounded by his memorabilia. Jack even had a tuft of grass encased as if it were the holy grail of the Dallas Cowboys. I bet that cost more than three bucks.

"Annette!" His shout broke my train of thought. Shit! How long had he been calling me?

"Coming. Just one minute," I responded. It was then that I remembered what I forgot. His snack. I'm always forgetting something. There I was crying over a drink that I didn't contribute to. Crying over my mistreatment. This man took an interest in me. He married me. He paid off all my bills, had to so I wouldn't affect his credit when we married. I grabbed a beer from the fridge and placed it in a cozy. Grabbed his Ridgies chips and french onion dip, placed it all on a tray and carried everything to his game room. He never asked me to join in. I didn't mind. I was never really into sports. I didn't understand it, and would hate for him to try to explain it to me. I pictured what he would say to his friends. He married a stupid woman who didn't understand football.

I set the tray down, and Jack didn't even look at me as he grabbed his beer. I stared at the coffee table, and my mind began to wander again. I remembered how he had kicked the table and slammed the sharp edge into my knee. It happened eight months ago, but how that moment still lingered in my mind. I'm sure that I wrote about this, but every time I see that coffee table I think of that moment, the moment that my best friend stood up to him. God, I miss her. I wish I had listened to her, but I thought that I was doing the right thing. What I would give to know where Deborah was. I wish I still had her phone number. Jack deleted it from my cell phone, and for some reason, she never called me again.

Deborah flew here to Dallas, Texas, from Rochester, New York, just for my wedding. I felt bad. I didn't put her in my wedding. I didn't think she would actually show. But she did. The way she acted reminded me that Deborah was my friend. She came when she really didn't need to, she couldn't even really afford to. But she did. She had a new baby that she was raising on her own. The reason why she came was apparent when I saw her. Deborah's once dark brown hair was now a bright pink. "This will be in all of your wedding pictures. This will be my silent protest." I was at first angry with her for this stunt, but I found that deep in my heart I was happy that she was strong enough to still speak her mind. "What happened to you?" I remembered her asking me. "Is his money really that important?" Deborah decided not to spend any more time in our house. She hated Jack. He called her insane for calling a cab and wasting money on a hotel. I'll never forget what she said to Jack. "I may be leaving your big ass house, but I will never leave Annette's life. You're nothing but a fucking phase!" Deborah stormed out of the house. Jack stormed upstairs. I followed him, and that is when the furniture flew. That is when the table hit my knee. That is when the blood gushed. I should have known better than to go after him. Thank God, my wedding dress would cover the wound. I did have to get stitches. Even today, my knee throbbed in pain, especially when it started to rain or if the temperature dropped. See how my head wanders. Just looking at a coffee table, I was consumed with other thoughts. I tried to act as if I hadn't been standing there for all that time staring at the coffee table.

Mop the floors, vacuum, and something else. "What do you want for dinner? I asked.

"Well, I think we should eat the leftovers from your pretend dinner party, unless there's more food you'd like to waste?" Jack threw his arms into the air. "You stupid fuck!" Jack screamed at the TV as he slammed the beer on the table next to him.

I turned to walk back down the stairs. I had to recite the list in my mind. Vacuum, mop the floors, reheat dinner...

"Annette," Jack said, "get started on the gutters. Storm's

heading our way tomorrow."

"Gutters, right." I walked down the stairs, but something still lingers in my mind. Hours later while he is asleep, and I am down in the laundry room scribbling in this diary, I know there is something else that I need to do. I just hope I remember before it's too late.

November 18th

Dear Diary,

Change the sheets, take a bath, and chill the wine. I did all those, but there was something else. I went through the day, doing these chores, but something was gnawing in the back of my mind. I wish I could remember what it was, that thing that was gnawing at me. I would welcome it, choose to be consumed by it. Anything would be better than doing the chores for this day. Today I started to ovulate, and fucking Jack to produce a child is my ultimate chore. He used to be fun, spontaneous. But now, sex is a duty, a job, a chore. Jack and I used to have amazing sex. That was one of the reasons I was so drawn to him. We used to tear our clothes off and fuck in random places—his truck, a filthy restroom, our backyard. Our passion was so strong. Our clothes ripped off, his head buried between my thighs. But now? He takes his time not between my thighs but rather taking off his clothes and folding them neatly, then setting them on the white wicker chair in the corner of our bedroom. I no longer see our passionate sweaty sex, but rather the thick black hair that covers his back and his ass. I hate body hair. Now I was married to this upholstered apish goon. He is no longer enticed by my face, my breasts, my vagina. No, he gets excited if I find a sale at the store, a way for us to save money. Even more depressing about today...it's my birthday, and I am expected to conceive. I didn't mention my birthday to him. After the week we had, I felt that I should just keep silent about it, but Jack came home with a dozen long-stemmed roses. I was surprised and angry. Then I felt guilty for feeling so angry. I know I told Jack about my ex-boyfriend. He would beat me senseless and always showed up with roses. I hated the scent of roses after that. Hated even the sight of them. I still hate them. When I see a rose, when I smell the scent of a rose, it brings me back to that time. I was pregnant, and my ex beat me. He was drunk and woke up thinking I was someone else. I don't know who he thought I was. All I know was that my ex was attacking me. He grabbed a picnic fork and stabbed me in the chest fourteen times. I lost the baby. But here was my husband with beautiful roses. Jack watched me as I arranged them in a vase. I tried to place them on the dining room table, but Jack wanted me to take them to the bedroom and place them on my dresser. It was so hard to trim those roses and put them in warm water in the vase. It was so hard to walk the roses over and place them on my dresser. I tried not to cry in our bedroom. I swallowed the knot in my throat once again as I walked downstairs.

Jack had his keys in hand and hugged me. He suggested that we go to the grocery store. He said that I could pick out whatever I wanted for dinner. He said that he would cook what I picked out for my birthday dinner. Jack always bought me beautiful clothes and jewelry, but food was a different story. I always had to eat what he wanted. I love fresh food. Jack was content to eat whatever was on sale. I was so excited; I could finally pick my meal. We drove to the store. I handpicked fresh green beans and mushrooms. I love sautéed mushrooms, but I also needed tomatoes, beefsteak tomatoes from the vine. I held the delicious fruit to my nose, sniffing it through its plump red skin, turning it over and lightly squeezing its silken flesh to make sure I picked the perfect red ruby tomato for my palate. I placed the mushrooms in the cart as well. Not just a package of them, but I had picked all six of them, large and plump, cherishing the velvety touch against the skin of my fingertips. Jack became antsy, shifting from side to side, sighing and huffing. I should have hurried. I should have moved faster, but for the first time in months, I was in the grocery store just for me. Everything in the cart was for my mouth's pleasure. It was my day. My special day. Maybe Jack could appreciate me. His huffing should have clued me in. I picked out a couple of fillets. Jack muttered that there was a sale on rib eye. I hate rib eye. They're so fatty. I wanted fillets. I looked at Jack and saw the vein throbbing in his forehead. He picked up the package of fillets and smacked me across the face. Smacked me. Right there in the middle of the grocery store. Right there in front of everyone. He left me there in the middle of the store, two miles from our house. I didn't have my purse, my car, or my keys. I had to walk.

LET THEM IN

It was an unseasonably hot day, and I had no water. My jaw still throbbed from being assaulted with my desired birthday steaks. I tried not to think of how thirsty I was. I tried to think of other things. My mind wandered to the fact that I was ovulating, then to Deborah. Thank God for her. She paid for me to go to the clinic, so I could have an IUD put in. I just couldn't deal with another bar on my cage—my sentence of life without parole—to be the constant dutiful wife and now doting mother. How long could I keep this up? I know Jack will become suspicious about my inability to conceive. Soon he'll take me to the doctor and insist on tests and fertility drugs. My heart pounded at the thought of them finding the device. Legally did they have the right to inform Jack that I had foiled his plans for a carbon copy?

I should just get away, but with what? I don't have any money. I was able to walk those two miles. Maybe I can get a job and just walk there. I can't take the car. Jack tracks my miles. But maybe I could get a job as a waitress and try to keep it secret. I would just have to be home before Jack. I would have to have all the chores done too. I would have to hide my money. How can I do this? I'm sad writing this right now. There is no way for me to get away with this. Jack knows everyone in town. I would be discovered. If only I had Deborah's phone number.

My situation was only worse when I arrived home. Jack ordered pizza and wings. I hate eating that shit. The grease upsets my stomach and always sends me to the bathroom. I ate my penance quietly as he stared at me. Time was ticking by, and I still had this chore to perform.

I changed the sheets, poured the wine, my body scented in a light fragrance of lilac from my bath. I stood next to the wine dressed only in my robe. It would be easy enough for me to take off, and I spared myself the torture of watching him neatly folding my clothes. I wished he would let me play some music. At least then I wouldn't have to listen to his grunts; at least then it would be easier for me to ignore his pathetic attempts at dirty talk. I downed a glass of wine, re-poured, and downed another. I tried not to sigh as Jack finished folding his underwear.

Then the nasty talk started. "Annette," he said walking towards me, "is it mean?"

"Yes, it's very mean." I pretended to stare at his dick, but I actually was staring at the floor. I just wanted to get this over with. Jack grabbed me by the hair and threw me on the bed.

It's so hard for me to write these words down, but I have to get them out. Maybe by writing down our dialogue I can get these phantom voices out of my head. How can a child be conceived out of such hatred? Deborah and I made sure that it wouldn't be. I can still hear his words in my head. The same shit he says every time he fucks me. We don't make love anymore. He just fucks me, and every time he says the same thing. Maybe by writing his words down I can dislodge them from my body. His nasty, ugly words that make me feel nasty and ugly:

"Tell me it's mean. Tell me you're scared of it."

Why did I share so much with him? Why did I tell him about

my past? Why did I tell him that I was raped when I was fourteen? It seems that my trauma was his fantasy, as if he was trying to relive some sick roleplay of being the man who took my virginity by force. I told him too much. I thought that I could trust him. He used my naivete against me. I am a stupid woman. I am surrounded by roses to remind me of the loss of my child, to remind me of the physical assault, to remind me of how I almost died. And now in the bedroom, he reminds me of the rape. He reminds me of how my parents didn't believe me. He reminds me of my mother striking me, of how she called me a whore. He reminds me of how my father institutionalized me. He repeats the words that fucker said to me so many years ago: *Is it mean?*

I wasn't lying when I said that it was mean. I wasn't lying when I said that I was scared. I closed my eyes. My head slammed against the headboard as I waited for the whole thing to be over with. A new list filled my head. I made sure to complete it after he fell asleep: Wash off Jack's scent, do the dinner dishes, swallow what was left of my pride. There was another thing I needed to do, but I forgot what it was. It would come to me eventually, at least I hoped that it would. Why can't I remember it? Maybe because there is so much to do. There is always so much to do.

November 19th

Dear Diary,

Today is the actual day of Jack's dinner party. All I wanted to do was disappear, to forget everything from yesterday at the grocery store, to forget Jack's fantasy rape last night. I didn't sleep at all. How could I? I could only think of what Jack did to me, and thinking about that drew me back to my past—the past that I wanted to bury for good, I had buried it for so long, but Jack had begged me to tell him everything, and now, that everything was foremost in my mind. My past was all I could think of.

I didn't want to wake him. I lay there silent as tears soaked my face and drenched the sides of my pillow. When his alarm went off, I flipped over my pillow and rolled on my side. I didn't want him to see my flushed cheeks and puffy eyes. I didn't want to hear what he had to say about the state I was in. How that state has changed, but I can't get ahead of myself. I have to get this down as it happened, otherwise I might forget.

I pretended to be asleep when his alarm went off. I waited until he got in the shower to get out of bed. I rushed to the downstairs bathroom and washed my face. I also put a dab of hemorrhoid cream under my eyes to take away the puffiness. I brewed the coffee and made his breakfast. I pretended to be researching recipes on my laptop when he came downstairs. He looked over my shoulder and snickered.

"Glad you're getting a head start on tonight. You'll have to outdo your practice run," he said as he shoveled his over-easy eggs in his mouth.

"I know tonight is important to you," I said.

"Do you?" He placed his dirty dishes in the sink. "I gotta go. Bills don't pay themselves." He didn't kiss me, didn't hug me, didn't even touch me as he grabbed his briefcase and walked out the front door.

I took a shower and winced as the hot water hit my vagina. I decided to forgo the underwear and opted to just wear baggy sweatpants and a sweatshirt to the store. My hair was in a ponytail. Sneakers on my feet. I grabbed a grocery cart and limped aimlessly around the Tom Thumb grocery store. I didn't know what I should make. I hadn't really looked anything up while he was eating his breakfast. The clock was ticking, and I was running out of time. I went to the meat department. That's where I should start. Forget about fresh vegetables. That's what I wanted. Jack loved his meat. I needed to go and decide on the carne. Seafood? Too light. Chicken? Too cheap. Beef? Too predictable. That's when I saw the perfect carne for Jack and his party. Lamb. I had never cooked lamb. I never had lamb. I've heard of it. It was a dish that was loved or hated. Peppermint jelly, rosemary, russet potatoes? Typical. I pulled out my cell phone. Google lamb recipes. Lamb chops sizzled with garlic...also called *Las Pedroneras*. Yes! This would be a hit over my practice run of beef Wellington. I grabbed all the ingredients. These were important clients. As much as my body ached, I rushed as fast I could through the grocery store. All this running around made me so thirsty, but I didn't dare grab a bottled water. I saw a drinking fountain and hesitated. I hated drinking from drinking fountains. They seemed so dirty to me, but my throat was dry, and I felt the sides of my mouth sticking to my tongue. I pressed the button on the fountain and lapped up the water.

I placed the groceries in the trunk of my car. No, not my car. That car was traded in for this blue Saturn. I had a car, a red Ford Mustang. According to Jack I was living beyond my means. I thought he was right. My payments were insane, and the insurance! I was siding with him, but then he said to me that no wife of his would drive a flashy car. He was so paranoid. He went off on men who looked at me. But Jack had paid for the reason that all of these men looked. He wanted me to have the implants. He wanted my breasts bigger. Honestly, I think my breasts are too big, but that was what Jack wanted. I slammed the groceries in the trunk of Jack's Saturn that he made me drive. I missed my old life. I missed my Mustang. I missed my saggy tits. I missed Deborah. I missed my freedom. Jack's words echoed in my head. I gripped the sides of my head as those words shouted in my mind: *You'll never leave me. You've become to accustomed to this life. Besides, I'd never sign the damn papers.*

I slammed the trunk down and grabbed my cell phone from my purse. Tears began to well in my eyes, and that knot ached in my throat again. I traced the numbers of my cell phone. God, I missed Deborah. I missed her laugh and her quirky way of commenting on life. Deborah would know what to do. She knew what to do at my wedding, but I didn't listen. This was my prince. Deborah saw right through him. Writing this all down, I know that she was right about him. Oh God, if anyone finds this diary, please know that I should have listened to her. I wish I had. But I didn't, and today I stood in the middle of Tom Thumb's parking lot caressing my phone thinking about what she said to me at my wedding reception: *Dude, we can leave. You wanna leave? Let's leave right now.* I didn't leave. I told Deborah to grow up. I told her that I didn't want to be like her, alone and miserable. I told her that she was just jealous of me and that an amazing man loves me. I told her that I was improving my life and that she could either get on board or get lost. She never spoke to me again. Now I am the one lost without her.

I snapped myself out of those thoughts. I had too much to do: wash the fine china, dust, vacuum, make dinner, and set up the bar. I had to make sure that everything was perfect—perfect house, perfect dinner, perfect drinks, perfect music. Perfect wife. Everyone, look at how perfect my husband is. He runs a tight ship. Now, he can run yours.

Jack, of course, landed the account. Glasses were raised. Men in suits smiled. Wives asked me for the recipe. Jack offered a meager nod of approval. The guests left, and I had to start my chores again. Clean the dining room, take out the trash, and clean the dishes. I washed the glasses first, then the plates. I was working on the silverware when Jack walked into the kitchen. He grabbed the dish towel. I thought that he was going to help me until he turned off the water. He took the towel and threw it at my chest. I caught the towel as he grabbed my shoulders and forced me to my knees.

"Congratulations are in order." He unzipped his pants. "Use the towel. I don't need an added mess in here."

"Jack, no."

"No?" he laughed at me holding my face. I was on my knees, dish bubbles clinging to my knuckles. "I said that congratulations are in order." His pants fell, and he tugged down his underwear. I tried to move away from his penis. He held me by the back of my head. "Open. Your. Mouth."

His penis was pressed against my lips. I started to sob. I couldn't stop. I looked around my kitchen. There were so many roses. He told his coworkers to bring them. He made me cut them and arrange them in vases, and now I was surrounded by them. The stench of them.

"It's not mean. It's been good to you," he said yanking my head back. "Now open your fucking mouth!"

I opened. I let him penetrate me. Let him. Did I have a choice? I was on my knees with him towering over me. He had my head in his hands, my hair enwrapped in his knuckles. I felt his dick in the back of my throat. My vagina was bruised and then he bruised my mouth and throat. "Say it's not mean. Say it's been good to you."

I couldn't say it. His dick was halfway down my throat. He gripped my hair harder and shoved my face into his pelvis. "Say it's not mean! Say it's been good to you!"

I gurgled past his pubic hair, "It's good. It's good."

"That's right." He pulled my head out and slammed it slowly against his pelvis. "Now say it's not mean."

I cried. I placed my hands against his thighs. "Please," I choked against his cock. "Please, Jack."

"Say it!" He slammed my head against his pelvis again.

I gurgled that it wasn't mean. He slammed my head repeatedly against him. His dick scraped the back of my throat. I threw up, but he didn't ease up. "Swallow it," he said. I bawled and snotted and threw up, and he made me swallow it all. He finally came, but he didn't pull out. He continued to ram me. A new mixture filled my mouth: snot, tears, vomit, and his sperm.

"Swallow it. Swallow it all!"

The towel was for nothing. He held my head tight. He lifted my chin up and watched me making sure that I did swallow it all. He came so much. I tried. I tried to swallow it, but I just couldn't. He held my chin up and looked in my tear-soaked eyes. My mascara ran down my cheeks. He laughed as he ran his fingers across my eyes.

"Swallow it, bitch. I'm not wasting my seed on your cunt anymore. Not until after your appointment." He threw me back against the cupboard. He zipped up and threw a card at my face. I remember sobbing. What else could I do but sob? I threw up. He grabbed me by the back of my head and placed my face in my vomit. "I said swallow it. Stick your tongue out and lick it up."

I had no choice. I began to lick it up. He picked up the card and pushed it in front of me. "You will get that device removed," he said. How did he know about it? What about HIPAA? Is there no protection for me? Am I nothing but a property? A breeder? "That's enough," he said. "I need a drink. Looking at you, you could use one too." Jack grabbed the wine glasses. "Open the Barco," he said.

I opened the bottle and poured wine in our glasses. He clinked his glass against mine and smiled. "You will go to your appointment and get that device removed. Did you think that I wouldn't find out? You will give me a child as per our agreement."

Agreement? Agreement? "Agreement? Jack this is a marriage, not one of your business ventures."

"Marriage is business, and you're failing miserably." He threw the wine glass in the sink. The glass shattered, shards flying out of the sink to the floor.

I looked at the roses in the vases. I smelled the air. I felt the knife penetrate my body. I felt my womb losing my child. I remembered Jack's penis. How it pressed against my face. I remembered how he made me lick his sperm and my vomit. I remembered my parents. I remembered how they didn't believe me. I heard the word whore. Jack turned and looked at me.

"My parents were right about you."

I was stuck. I was trapped. I could never make him happy. I could never please his family. He would always make excuses to his friends as to why I am his wife. I didn't want to give him a child, and now he had found me out. He knew my secret. I looked at the vomit on the floor mixed in with his semen. I looked at the dishes. I looked at the food that still needed to be put away. I started to dry heave. Jack just laughed.

No. No more bars. I counted down in my head: five, four, three, two, one... clean the dining room, put away the food, wash the dishes, go to this appointment...No!

"I thought I could raise you up," he said, "but a pig is a pig."

I couldn't help myself. I gripped the wine opener in my hands. He took a deep sip of his wine, and as he did so I drove the corkscrew in the side of his neck. Blood spurted all over my apron. Blood shot on the white tiled floor. He tried to grip the corkscrew, but there was so much blood. I pulled the wine tool from his neck and drove it into his temple. He fell to the floor, and I plummeted with him. I drove the wine tool into his throat over and over and over again. I plunged it into Jack until he stopped moving.

I now lift my bloodied hands in the air. I slapped myself, and I continue to slap myself as I write this entry. I must get myself together.

Dishes, clean up the dining room, put the food away, drag Jack into his car and push it over a cliff. He has to be totally burned. They can't see the punctures in his skin. Make sure it explodes. Deborah loved crime shows. Why can't I remember her number!? Get rid of him. That's what I kept forgetting. This is what I am supposed to do. I can be so stupid sometimes. Maybe his parents were right. Maybe he should have married a Baylor girl. She would have done this a long time ago. I need to shake this off. I need to clean myself up. I need to burn this journal. Oh my God, I have so much to do. I feel so stupid. The evidence. The clean-up. Snap out of it. I don't have time for these thoughts when there is so much to do.

VAMP

You say "Hi" and I say "Hi" back. What should we talk about? Should we talk about our escapades one more time? Should we send each other another photo, another selfie, of us alone in the setting, the background. This is me at work, alone. This is me at my kitchen table, alone. This is me in my car, alone. This is me in my bed thinking of you, alone. And now I am here in my room, alone. My phone at my ear as I hear you breathing. There is no speech. No small talk. No chatter. Just your breath. And I am on my bed, listening to your breath as I feel you in me.

"Hi," you say.

"Hi," I say back. My vision is not blurred or disrupted. My eyes are shut tight. I feel your fingers caressing my face, my forehead, my cheekbones, my neck, then my shoulders. I feel your hands on my breasts. I feel you delve into me. Fingers at first and then.

I breathe. You breathe back. There is nothing but our steady breathing, balancing the thousand miles between us. In. Then out.

In. Then out. My body shakes as you enter me with the sound of your breath through my phone. I hear you moan. I'm in my bed, my hands at my head. I feel you inside of me, whispering to me, "Hi."

I moan into the phone a whimper.

You moan back just enjoying me. You say, "I can't wait to have you. All of you."

I feel a swirling force of torridity flow from my insides, beginning with my pussy, into my stomach, touching my breasts, touching my hard nipples, filling my throat until I moan again. I start to laugh. You laugh back. I stretch out in my bed, sheets soaked with my cum. I feel cold and pull the blankets around me.

"I have to go," I say as I shake against the sweat trapped in my sheets.

You tell me good night, but I still feel you there in my bed. I try different positions: on my back, stomach, left, the right side. Yet there you remain still thrusting inside of me. I grab my phone and search YouTube for the thunder and lightning sounds. Positive and negative draw together inside of clouds releasing the crash. With those crashes, I finally fall asleep.

I slept through my alarm. I was supposed to get up early. The stairs needed a good vacuuming. The downstairs floors needed to be swept and mopped. The walls in the kitchen needed to be scrubbed. I almost choked as I attempted to get out of bed. I found myself wrapped in my blankets. The sheets were wrapped around my neck. I pulled at my sheets and blankets as I struggled to release myself from my bed.

I was finally at the stairs. My body was sore, muscles in my thighs predicting a charley horse at any moment. I fumbled my way down the stairs and limped to the bathroom. *Just pee and brush your teeth.* I rinsed and spit in the sink. I looked in the mirror. My cheeks were florid. And my eyes. I pulled off my glasses and looked at myself in the mirror. Dark circles under my bloodshot eyes. The circles so dark as if I had been struck. The muscles in my thighs tensed up ready to release a shooting spasmic pain. I breathed in. I breathed out. I opened the bathroom door and crawled up the stairs to my bedroom. I held myself, my arms wrapping around my shoulders, knees drawn to my chest. My phone pinged. It was you.

"Babe, you alright?"

THE CIRCLE

Deidre chose to run down the slate walk rather than feel trapped inside her aunt's Victorian house filled with cobwebs and faded yellow doilies. She stopped when she reached a wooded area lined with chrysanthemums and daylilies. Although she wanted to keep running through the woods filled with decaying grape vines. The delicate flowers opening their petals to feel the heat of the sun were too inviting to Deidre. She sat next to a patch of daylilies and rubbed her nose against the soft velvet petals. Deidre knew the flowers were right. She should just sit down and relax. Aunt Clara was her last and only hope. If she failed here, Deidre would wind up in one of three places: rehab, jail, or a cemetery. She crawled to an elder tree, nestled herself against the crook of the trunk and traced its rugged skin with her fingertips. Deidre breathed deeply, knowing she had to return to the house, knowing this place was the only dwelling she could call home. It was bad enough to be trapped with this old woman, to be taken from her friends, but the hallucinations weren't aiding her sobriety. The images of fires and decaying flesh sometimes snuck into her peripheral vision, making her think that she was still trapped in a K-hole.

Deidre lay there until the sun set. She missed dinner again. Aunt Clara left a plate of food on the kitchen table. Deidre scribbled a thank you on the dry erase board that hung on the vintage, red Northstar fridge and slopped the food down the garbage disposal. Her stomach still churned at the thought of food. A hot bath would serve as a placebo for her excited nerves.

The one thing she did love from Clara's house was her old-fashioned bathtub. It was porcelain with claw feet. The tub was deep and long. She didn't care for the black and white checkered floor or for the peeling floral wallpaper, but with a tub like that, who cared about the scenery? Not an inch of her body was exposed as she lay under the bubbles swishing around. She lifted her legs and extended her toes to the top of the tub. Her brown hair floated in the small waves her body created in the bubbly water. Her pores opened from the heat of the bath as she watched the steam rise to the ceiling lamp and disappear. The washcloth slid with a "plop" in the water. Deidre picked up the cloth, wrung it out, and put it back on her face.

"Deidre." She heard his voice and felt movement in the water. Deidre yanked the washcloth from her face. Justin sat in front of her, his knees drawn to his chin, the water soaking his blue jeans and white, woolen sweater. He held a razor blade in his hand. Deidre grabbed at his hand, but she passed through him like the vapor disappearing beneath the bathroom light.

"Don't." She tried to grab his hand again, but her fingers passed through him and touched the brass fixtures behind him.

"But this is what you wanted me to do. He lifted the razor and sliced his arms. The blood pumped from his veins, and the red liquid swirled in her lemongrass scented bathwater. Justin's head bobbed up and down in the murky water. Deidre toppled over the side of the bathtub and pulled the towel to her face.

Deidre hadn't meant what she said to him. Justin had had another bad day at the animal shelter. No one adopted his favorite alley cat, Lucky. Justin begged her to let him bring Lucky home. Deidre refused, and Justin watched them put Lucky down. That's when the fighting intensified. Deidre just couldn't let him bring home another animal. They already had two cats, a dog, and a smelly turtle. After Lucky was put down, Justin lashed out at her. She tried to calm him down, tried to tell him that they couldn't rescue every animal slotted to die. He struck her. Deidre stormed off and threw some clothes in her backpack.

"Where are you going?" Justin had tried to stand in her way.

Deidre pushed past him. "Not staying here with you, with this. I need some space."

"Don't leave me." Justin got on his knees. He held her waist and placed his head on her abdomen. "I'm so sorry. I shouldn't have hit you."

Deidre pushed him off. "But you did."

"You leave, I have nothing. I can't do this alone. I can't be alone."

Deidre opened the front door.

"I'll end it." The same threat Justin always used when they had a fight. Deidre snickered and turned to him.

"Do it. Go be with Lucky." She never thought he would follow through with it. He had made the same threats every time she tried to leave him, even if it was just to get some space. But he did do it. He killed himself. Deidre returned home after being away for three days to see the same scene that was before her now.

Deidre snapped back to the present. "You're not real." Her breathing became heavy as she pulled the bath towel away from her eyes. He lay still in the tub full of crimson water. "It's in my head. Just in my head." She placed her fingertips on the edge of the porcelain tub and peered at his still body.

Justin opened his eyes. "I'm waiting for you."

Deidre grabbed the towel and covered her mouth, as she watched Justin's body slowly disappear, taking the red with him. All that was left was her fluffy bubbles and the humming sound of the overhead light.

*　　*　　*

As usual, there was an assortment of herbal teas on the kitchen table. Deidre thumbed through them and tapped a tarnished silver spoon against her teacup. Would it kill her aunt to allow some form of chemical? Deidre would kill for a cup of coffee.

"Be careful with that cup. It's an antique."

"Just like everything else around here," Deidre muttered.

"At some point today, I have to get those blankets finished for the troops," Clara said ignoring Deidre's last comment. "Those poor men serving under that miscreant. I never thought I would see the day when a black man would run this country. Oh, if only Dick Cheney's heart wasn't a problem. He would've made a great president."

"He shot a man." Deidre couldn't believe they were related.

"It was an accident. Sleep well?"

"Not exactly."

Clara leaned against the window, the sunlight illuminating the silver hairs of her head. "Deidre, I know this is hard on you, but I think it's what's best for you. If your father had let me take you after your mother passed on, maybe you wouldn't be in the position you're in now." She tossed a ham steak in the frying pan. "Honestly, I don't know what your father was thinking trying to raise a newborn on his own." She stared at her niece. "You look so much like your mother. It must have been hard on your father to be reminded of her."

Once again, Clara brought up Deidre's mother. Clara never said her mother's name. Diana. She only referred to her as *your mother*. Deidre's mother was from Spanish Town, Jamaica. Her parents met in Toronto, Canada. They fell immediately in love, much to Clara's dismay. Diana's long hair was so kinky and her velvety skin so dark. What if they had children? They only had one. Diana was involved in a car accident. They were able to save Deidre, but not her mother. Clara's words always hurt her, and now she was stuck here in this old house with this old racist woman. Deidre stood up.

"Where are you going?" Clara asked.

"I'm not hungry."

"Oh no, I made your favorite, ham and over-easy eggs. You always asked me to make it for you when you were little."

"I'm not little anymore."

"No, you're not, but you're going to sit down and you're going to eat." Clara led Deidre back to the table and set her breakfast in front of her. "Now, I'm going to sit here and make sure you eat your breakfast. No more dumping my good cooking down the garbage disposal."

Deidre forced the food into her mouth, anything to shut her aunt up.

"Just look at you, skin and bones. That's no way to keep a man. A man needs curves. Poor Justin."

Deidre slammed her fork on the table. Clara jumped at the sound. Deidre pushed the plate away from her. "Goddammit. Really, Aunt Clara?"

Clara cleared her throat. "Language," she said as she got up and went to the sink. "I was just making an observation." Clara started washing the frying pan. Deidre decided to eat the rest of her breakfast. There was no use in fighting. She shoved a forkful of eggs in her mouth and glared at her aunt. That's when she noticed it, the pale fingertips gripping the edge of her aunt's red and white polka dot apron. Her gaze followed the fingertips and saw a woman with stringy, black hair floating an inch above the floor. Her pupils were opaque. She had a nose piercing and a tattoo of a fairy on her shoulder. Clara walked to the kitchen table, and the woman moved effortlessly with her as if she was made of air, floating around Clara's apron like a down feather. The woman opened her mouth. Deidre expected a scream, but there was no sound, just the woman's gaping mouth and blackened teeth.

* * *

Deidre heard the bedroom door lock behind her. It was Clara's naptime, and, therefore, it was Deidre's naptime as well. She sat on her bed, her knees drawn to her chin. She couldn't get the image of that woman out of her head. She wished she could think of something else, have something to distract her. If only Deidre could get to her laptop or phone, but Aunt Clara kept those under lock and key as well. It had been so long since she had seen the outside world. She had lost track of the days. There was no use dwelling on friends she couldn't see, to dwell on a boyfriend who chose to kill himself, or whatever that woman was in the kitchen. It had to be a hallucination. Deidre decided to close her eyes and go to sleep.

When Deirdre opened her eyes, the sun had set. She had managed to sleep another day away. The sky was overcast, keeping the moonlight from her. She reached for her lamp, fumbling for the cord. In the corner, she heard footsteps shuffling on the floor. "Aunt Clara?" No voice responded. Deidre swallowed and held her body still in the stark darkness. She felt pressure on her mattress as if someone had sat beside her. She heard breathing. Felt a hand on her leg, and a draft of cold air as the breathing deepened. Lips touched her shoulder. She felt hair against her cheek. Deidre's hand shook as she again reached for the light cord. A hand grabbed her arm, the grip, harsh, drawing her arm down.

"Justin?"

"You didn't come to me," Justin whispered in her ear. "I've waited so long for you to come to me." She felt him kiss her cheek. His lips grazed her ear as he followed the goose bumped flesh of her neck. She felt his grip tighten on her thigh, his fingers pushing the fabric of her dress aside, sliding his fingertips to her inner thigh. "I'm tired of waiting."

Deidre felt repulsed by the touch of his cold hands against her skin. But the more he breathed in her ear, the more she wanted to spread her legs and let the dead man in. A key was pressed in the lock. The door knob turned.

His other hand clutched her breast. "It won't be much longer," he said, kissing her lips.

The door opened. "Deidre, supper's ready." Clara walked to the lamp and turned it on. Deidre sat on the bed staring at the wall. "How long have you been sitting in the dark?"

"I just woke up." Deidre looked around the room, but there was no sign of Justin.

"Well, come and eat." Clara left the room. Deidre sat for a moment on the bed. She had felt his touch, heard his voice. She needed to keep this knowledge to herself.

Moments of silence passed as Clara and Deidre ate together. Lately, eating seemed to be the only thing Clara did. Clara chewed her last bite of spaghetti, set her fork and spoon down, and gazed at Deidre. "You really are such a pretty thing. A couple of good meals, and already the glow has returned to you."

"Thank you, I think." Deidre forced a smile.

"Well, you are. It would be a shame to let all that beauty go to waste."

Clara walked to the fridge and brought out a bottle of Riesling. She handed Deidre a glass.

"Aunt Clara, you know that I'm not supposed to have this."

Clara waved her hand at her. "I've been hard on you, I admit. Sometimes, I don't know what to say to you. And what has been coming out of my mouth lately has been less than kind." She lifted her glass. "To a new beginning."

Deidre greeted her glass and took a sip of the wine. "Thank you, Aunt Clara."

"It has to be so lonely here for you. I should be more understanding." Clara sipped her wine and relaxed in the chair. "I'll be more lenient in some ways; just keep in mind I made your father a promise to watch over you."

"It's my fault, being here. I'm sorry to be such a burden."

"No, you're not a burden at all. And you had a moment of weakness. Honey, your fiancé killed himself. Your father wasn't there for you, and I didn't even know you were engaged. It's no wonder you self-medicated. I just wish there was someone there for you. That I was there for you. Here I am, constantly busy with charity work, and I neglected my own family." Clara stared at Deidre.

Deidre caught her aunt's gaze and looked away. When she looked back Clara still gawked at her. "What?"

"I guess I just didn't realize until now how beautiful you are. You have such potential, if only you could see that."

"I must get it from you." Deidre felt uneasy about her aunt's new resolve to be her friend, but she decided to play nice. "You look half your age."

Clara poured Deidre another glass. "No, just expensive creams. Did you know how nourishing a placenta is to our skin?"

Deidre wrinkled her nose at the thought of Clara rubbing creams made of placentas on her face.

"While you were in your room I have had some time to think. And I think maybe less restrictions and a little more understanding would be more beneficial to you." Clara drank the remainder of her wine. "However, you have to stay on the property. Youth today need a distraction. Would you like to watch something?" Clara stood up taking the bottle of wine with her.

"You don't have a television." Deidre followed her aunt through the kitchen and down the hallway. Clara pulled out a key and unlocked the basement door. Deidre followed Clara down the stairs and saw a finished basement. Clara led Deidre to a plush leather couch. The basement was such a stark contrast to the rest of the house. There was a fifty-eight-inch flat screen TV mounted to the wall. There was a drop ceiling and the walls were redone. There was even a Megan Duncanson print on one wall. It caught Deidre's eye. A landscape piece of a barren tree set against vivid colors of blue, orange, and red.

"I know how much you like her work. It was in your journal."

"You read my journal?" Deidre turned.

"I know it's an invasion, but I didn't know who you were."

"You could have asked."

"You were such a mess when you got here. I didn't know what to do. I wanted to surprise you. I did this all for you, set it up while you were taking your naps." Clara walked to Deidre. "Please don't be angry with me. Your father begged me to help you. If he wasn't so ill, he would have taken you in. I admit, I wasn't happy in the beginning. I had a certain way I did things. I never had children, never had to take care of anyone but myself. Please accept this room as my sincerest apology."

"I want my things back: my clothes, my journal, my laptop, and my phone."

"I don't know if that's a good idea. Your recovery."

"Aunt Clara, I'm not going to get better if you don't start trusting me. It was a bender. I was depressed about Justin. It was a stupid mistake."

"You almost overdosed."

"Because I was depressed, and I didn't know what the hell I was doing. I didn't know you couldn't mix those drugs. It was stupid, not intentional."

Clara walked to Deidre. "I'll go and get your clothes and journal out of storage tomorrow. I didn't keep your things here. I'm sorry, but I didn't trust you when you moved here. I didn't know what to do."

"And my laptop? My phone?"

"Let's build up to that." Aunt Clara kissed Deidre on the cheek. "You really are a special girl. Don't forget that." She turned to leave. "For now, just enjoy the television. I don't know the channels, but the cable man said that you can access the guide."

As pissed as she was at her aunt, Deidre could not resist the TV. It had been so long since she had seen anything other than her aunt and those damn blankets she knotted. She couldn't believe that her first pick was the news. She watched the scenes unfold before her. Nothing had changed, really. As she rested on the couch, her vision seemed blurred. Image ran into image—a collage of human misery mucked on the large screen before her. She heard the angry shouting of Afghanis, heard the happy cries of sports fans. Shouts and cheers. Humanity was a loud blur of technicolored noise. The image on the screen skipped and jumped. Probably just a storm messing with the signal. Deidre changed the channel, but that one was pixelating as well. She heard a loud hum as the picture jumped so fiercely that it appeared to be caught in a strobe. The image went hazy. Smoke spiraled in the air from the screen. Then she saw her. The dead woman from the kitchen. The pale thing pointed to a cabinet next to the fridge. Deidre couldn't move. The woman, her limbs twisting and convulsing, floated towards her. Deidre tried to bury herself in the couch digging her toes under the pillows of the sofa. The woman moved towards Deidre until she felt the dampness of her blood-soaked clothes and her cold skin against her body. Deidre found herself trapped on the couch. The woman once again pointed to the cabinet. Deidre closed her eyes. She wouldn't see this thing, wouldn't acknowledge it. She felt a cold hand on her chin yanking her head to the direction of the cabinet. Fingers pried Deidre's eyelids open, and she had no choice but to look. The woman stood in front of the cabinet and opened her mouth. A low guttural howl, like the sound of a wounded wolf would make, came out of her.

"No, no, no. You're not real." Deidre looked away. "You're not real. This is just in my head." The woman appeared in front of her and moved as if her joints were broken. She lifted her stringy hair from her neck showing Deidre a gaping hole leaking blackened blood. The woman advanced. Grabbed Deidre by the throat. Pushed Deidre to the couch. "Look," the woman said then disappeared.

Deidre shook against the couch cushions and grabbed her throat. Her chest heaved as she wiped the cold sweat from her forehead. This was no hallucination. Something was seriously wrong with Aunt Clara's house. She forced herself to have the nerve to walk to the cabinet. She hoped that there would be nothing there but plastic cups and dish detergent. She hoped this was all in her head. She needed to open the cabinet and see that there was nothing there, face her hallucinations and come to grips with the fact that perhaps she had done permanent damage to her brain.

Of course, Aunt Clara had locked the cabinet. Deidre looked around for something to pry it open with. She found an old tool box under the sink and grabbed a hammer. She pried open the cabinet door, splintering the wood in the process. No dish detergent, no plastic cups, just an old shoe box. Inside were badges of nurses and several driver's licenses. They were all of women in their early twenties. One of the badges was identical to the pale woman she saw in the kitchen. She dug deeper and found newspaper clippings reporting the disappearances of women stemming back to 1976. There had to be at least twenty ids in the shoe box. Alleghany county, Wayne, Mt. Morris, Rochester. She threw the ids on the table. The woman appeared again.

"Get out," the woman said. "Run."

Deidre bolted up the stairs and pushed open the door. She saw a rolling pin swing in the air, felt an explosion in her head, and fell backwards down the stairs.

*　*　*

Deidre touched her throbbing head and realized that her hands were tied together. Her clothes had been removed, and she was covered in rope knotted at certain points of her body. The ropes ran to the ceiling through a pulley system over the porcelain tub. The bathroom was lit in rows of candles. There was an altar at the tub. She winced from the pain in her forehead and squinted to see the altar clearer. A picture of Justin was on the altar and what appeared to be his boxer shorts. Deidre remembered those boxers. She had given them to him on Valentine's Day. A female figure approached her. She knew this was no hallucination as Aunt Clara's physique loomed into view.

Clara rubbed Deidre's forehead with her hand and licked the blood from her fingertips. Deidre wriggled against her bindings. "It wasn't supposed to come to this." Aunt Clara pulled a knife from her apron. "You were supposed to be passed out. Guess the sleeping pills I put in that wine didn't take, but I've learned that nothing really goes according to plan."

Deidre continued to struggle against the heavy rope that bound her. "So, this new beginning was all bullshit."

"Language."

"Fuck you." Deidre spit in Clara's face.

Clara wiped her face with her apron. "Oh, you can grant beauty, but you can't always grant grace." She set the knife on the edge of the tub and turned on the water. The steam filled the room. Clara whispered something strange as the water filled the tub. Deidre's vision began to clear, regardless of the steam. She saw the water shift as small waves moved back and forth. The water in the tub filled with swirling crimson water. Justin sat there smiling up at her.

"I told you it would be soon," he said.

"I know you did," Deidre replied.

Clara looked at the tub and smiled. "Oh good, you're here."

"You can see him?" Deidre started to cry.

"Oh, honey, I brought him here." Clara looked at the altar then back at Deidre. "I may be a killer, but I can't be heartless, not to my kin. You deserve to be happy, even after you're dead." Clara walked to the altar. "I called him here. It's better to be surrounded by someone you love. Trust me, I see how being alone affects those girls I killed. Can't have that happening to you." Clara began to undress in front of the altar.

Deidre heard a shuffling by the bathroom door. The woman was back. The woman glared at Clara who continued to disrobe. "I told you to run," the woman said looking at Deidre as she moved in circles around Aunt Clara. She acted as if she wanted to kill Clara, but she refused to touch her. Maybe she couldn't touch her, but Justin touched Deidre. Maybe it's different with this woman. What had Clara done to her? What was Clara going to do to Deidre?

Aunt Clara turned and stood naked in front of her. Her breasts were firm, but her stomach was wrinkled. She had cellulite and varicose veins on one thigh, but the other leg was the perfect rendition of a twenty-year-old woman. "Those creams can only do so much. The blood of the living, that's the key. Strangers are okay, but kin, that's the real secret to youth." Clara pulled on the rope, hoisting Deidre off the ground. Deidre screamed. She caught sight of the knife on the edge of the tub. Clara, busy with the hoisting, didn't notice it, maybe didn't remember it. She was repairing her body through these murders, but her mind was forgetful. Deidre grabbed the knife with her bound hands. She gripped it tight.

"I just need your blood. Then I'll be whole again."

"The food? The wine?" Deidre had to keep her aunt distracted.

"Had to fatten you up. And tonight? Every sacrifice deserves a last hoorah. Now hold still. I'll make it quick." Aunt Clara looked for the knife but didn't see it. She looked up at her niece. Deidre plunged the knife into her aunt's eyeball, driving it in her brain. She held on as the old woman struggled. Clara's hands flew up and scratched at Deidre's face. Deidre pulled her head back from Clara's fingernails. Clara's body jerked as if she were having a seizure then slowly fell limp. Her head slid off the knife as her body fell to the tub.

"No..." Justin said. "Forever. That's what she promised."

Deidre hung upside down with the knife still in her hands. She needed to cut herself down, but all she could do was stare at Justin. "I am so sorry," Deidre said. "But you really need to move on."

THE MOSQUITO

My stalker stood steadfast underneath the dancing branches of a willow tree. My feet kept their usual pace as my wooden clogs crisply fell on the white pavement of the sidewalk. He began to shake, his body embarking on its transformation. My ex-boyfriend's arms and legs shrank, and little hairs protruded from his pasty skin. Frail antennas thrust forth from his temples, and dismal wings unfolded through his shoulder blades. Unnerved, I kept my pace and rounded the corner of my street. I heard the annoying buzz-buzz of his undying chatter as he whipped past my ear seeking to bite me once again and leave me red and itchy, another one of his quaint victories. My hand embraced the aluminum can. I turned and pressed the nozzle and let the fluid gush into the air. His squirming, puny body twisted with the poisons of the insect repellant as he fell convulsing on the pavement. *Thwap! Swoosh!* I dragged the carcass of my mosquito across the pavement with my pretty, wooden clogs.

REFLECTION

"Got a fag?" the stranger asked Andria as he approached her.

"A what?" Andria inched backwards and felt the concrete wall behind her.

"A fag. You're smoking one now." He kept approaching. "Do you not know what you're smoking?"

"Oh, you want a cigarette." Andria reached in her purse, took out a pack of Marlboro Lights, and handed the stranger a cigarette.

He took the cigarette from her long fingers and smelled it. "Got a light? I normally don't smoke, but I need a fag when I'm this pissed."

Andria lit his cigarette and looked at him strangely.

He must have caught her befuddlement because he sighed. "Ugh, drunk. I'm not angry. I need a *cigarette* when I'm this *drunk.*"

"Sorry, but you took me off guard. You sound Irish. I thought only Brits said fag."

"I'm a bit of this, bit of that, really." The stranger took a drag off his cigarette. "Oh, that's perfect." He took another drag and blew the smoke above their heads. "I needed that. Name's Gan. You?"

"Andria."

"Andria, Andria. That's a pretty name."

"Thanks. Gan, that's different." She finally looked at him. He was tall and toned. She could see the muscles of his arms under his t-shirt. His brown hair was cut close, almost military style, and his eyes were a deep, warm brown. His skin was what unnerved her. It was so tan and his accent so Irish. "Definitely different."

"What's your meaning?"

"You just don't look Irish."

"Ha ha. Suppose only Americans can be mixed breeds? My ma's Sicilian. I was born in Palermo but raised in Dublin."

"And your father?" Andria asked.

"From Dublin. When I was five, Ma passed away. Da passed a few years back. Went to London to see my sister. Cunt she was, and here I am. Do you need more information for this fag?"

"No." Andria wanted to light another cigarette, but then she would have to be outside longer with Gan. He was very handsome, but something about his demeanor unnerved her. She should just go back in the bar. "I didn't mean to intrude. Sorry."

"It's behind us. No serious talk. Just a handshake. I thank you for the fag." Gan held out his hand. Andria felt repelled by this gesture, but she didn't know why. There was nothing wrong with it. His hand was perfectly normal. His brown eyes appeared innocent.

His accent succulent. His looks appealing, but for some reason touching his hand felt inappropriate. "It's just a hand, sweetie. Not gonna hurt you."

"Sorry," she said. She accepted his hand in hers. Her fingers felt like limp noodles boiled too long. Her heart beat like hummingbird wings. Gan drew her in and placed his arm over her shoulder. "Maybe I'm a bit pissed too," she whispered.

"No worries, sweetie. I'm here. Let's go in and get some whiskey." Gan walked Andria back in the bar, not letting go of her hand, not releasing her shoulder, his lips still nuzzling her ear.

Andria could no longer hear the music. She could no longer understand the words. She had lost sight of her friends. All she could make out was Gan. He was so clear in front of her. She could discern every detail. She could see the detail of his skin, the mole on his cheek, the freckles on his nose, the wisp of gray in his side burns. Trying to look away from him made Andria feel sick. The environment around her blurred when she even tried to look away from those eyes. How many shots had it been? Five? Six? And what was in that flask? She needed her bed. She needed to throw up. She needed to call in to work tomorrow.

"I gotta go. I gotta go." Andria attempted to stand and stumbled. Gan held her up as last call was called.

"Whoa there, sweetie." Gan kissed her cheek. He looked at the bartender. "Check, please. We won't be needing anything more." He held Andria up as she dug around in her purse for her keys. He took the keys from her. Andria attempted to grab the keys back but instead hiccupped letting loose pre-vomit spittle from her lips. Gan grabbed a napkin and wiped her mouth. "Let's call you an Uber." Andria looked at him and started laughing. "That's funny? That I know what an Uber is? Can you tell the cabby where you live?"

"I'm, I'm, uh. I live."

"Thought so. I'll drive." The bartender returned with the check, and Gan paid it. He scooted Andria away from the bar and held her wobbly body as they exited the bar. Gan looked at Andria's feet and sighed. "You really shouldn't wear those shoes. You're tall enough. They don't help you."

"I like my shoes." Andria's right heel caught on a crack in the sidewalk. She broke loose from Gan's grasp and fell to the pavement. The concrete scraped her skin, and blood gushed from her knees. Gan picked her up and carried her to his Ford pickup. He kissed her ear and her cheek. He tried to hush her as she moaned and cried from the pain.

They managed to find her house. Andria didn't apologize for how it looked. The dishes were piled in the sink. Laundry was piled up in the corner of her bedroom. Cigarettes in the ashtrays. Ashes all over her night stand. Gan overlooked it all. He had to find bandages, sanitizer, antibiotics. He dressed Andria's wounds, redressed her in a baggy t-shirt, and put her to bed. He didn't leave. He should have. He laid next to her fully dressed. Andria woke up. She turned to him and kissed him.

"Take off your clothes," she said.

"No. You're wasted."

"I want you inside me."

"And I don't want the cops at my door tomorrow with charges of rape." He kissed her cheek. "You're drunk." He kissed her again and brushed her long bangs out of her eyes. Her tears streamed mascara from her eyes. He wiped the black tears from her face. "Sweetie, I love what you've done with your makeup."

Andria laughed. Gan chuckled back as he kissed her cheek again. "You're so beautiful," he said. "Even with your Heath Ledger Joker eyes."

"You say the nicest things."

Gan got up.

"Where are you going?" Andria asked.

"Be right back." Gan found her bathroom. He took a washcloth off the shelf and ran the water until it was warm. He soaked the washcloth, wrung it out, and returned to the bedroom. "Let's clean you up," he said. But Andria had passed out. He smiled at her and gently wiped the mascara from her face. He set the makeup-stained washcloth on her nightstand and scooted down the bed, so his face was next to hers. He touched her nose and smiled. "That's better."

He watched her sleep. She let out little moans as she scraped her top teeth on her bottom lip. Her lips were beautiful. Full at the bottom lip, with her top lip dipped low, they created a heart shape on her face. He should leave, but he couldn't. All he could do was lie there and watch her sleep, listen to her moan. This wasn't what Gan did. He didn't get involved. He bedded them, and he left them. He couldn't do that with Andria. Her moans began to form words, and he listened to her talk in her sleep. At first, she said, "I'm so sorry." She repeated those words seven times. Gan counted them on his fingers. Then she said, "Dirty. Disgusting." Those words she repeated only three times.

He knew she was damaged. That's why he had picked her. He should have already fucked her, but for some reason he waited. He couldn't push back the hunger that was rising within him. When tears formed behind her closed eyelids, his arousal peaked. He got up and paced the room as Andria moaned about her rotten life. He walked to her dresser and looked in the mirror. "Leave. You should leave now." He was drawing this from her, as he drew all the pain from the women he had bedded before. Gan couldn't understand why it was so different now.

"Die. I wanted to die. I should die," Andria muttered as she rolled on her side.

Those words piqued his excitement. They were the words he needed to hear. He was there to do one job: make her confess, bed her, and drive her to her maddening end. His body obeyed her words. His cock swelled. "Fuck you," he said into the mirror. He looked at her bedroom door. He wanted to run through it and find a way out, but his body would not be denied. He needed to be inside her. He needed to feel her pain, feed from it. He needed to usher her to her grave. Gan spit on the mirror and punched the side of his head. He took in a breath and took off his clothes. He looked at his naked body in her mirror. "Fuck you," he said again. He turned to her bed and looked at Andria as she flipped on her back. She was still asleep. She pulled the blankets off her body, her hands lifting her t-shirt exposing her breasts. The cool air of her apartment immediately made her nipples hard. She spread her legs. Gan ran his fingers through his hair. He held his jaw as he looked at her writhing body. It was time. It was time for her last confession.

Gan crawled into bed with her. He licked her tears and kissed her cheeks. He listened to the vile things that spewed from her lips. Gan took it all in. He wiped a tear from his eye. These women never made him cry before. Andria had been abused. She spoke of a man her mother had let move into their house. She spoke of how he violated her. She was only eleven. Andria stopped talking. Gan nuzzled her ear. "I want to know you. I want to know all of you," he said as he wiped the tears from his eyes. Andria began to shake. Gan held her close to his naked flesh. He felt his energy leave his solar plexus and enter hers. She stopped shaking, stopped fighting him. Her lips began to move again. She was living a lie. She was selling a lie. She had a lucrative business as a wedding planner, but she had destroyed marriages. Affairs. Even prostitution. That's how she had the money to start her business. Give women their perfect day and fuck the husband to be. She couldn't help herself.

Instinct. Andria worked off instinct. Her instinct lashed out due to the damage that had been done. "Tell me everything," Gan said. "Tell me everything you have done." Andria obeyed. She told Gan of the one night she cut herself. She had to wear long sleeves for almost a month to hide her self-loathing. She told him how she hadn't done it since, but that she missed the release it gave her—

trading the emotional pain for the physical. How she was so numb that physical pain made her feel alive again.

Andria's eyes finally opened. Gan was on top of her. Gan had a hold of her hands and pinned them above her head. Gan kissed her on the lips. She opened to him accepting his tongue in her mouth. "Do you still want me inside you?" Gan asked.

"Yes," Andria breathed.

Gan pushed himself inside her. His barbs shot out of his cock and attached to the walls of her vagina. Andria screamed, beating his back with her fists. "I know. I know," he said as he held her tight. "But I need your pain." Gan buried his head in her long, red hair.

"This hurts. This hurts."

Gan thrust deeper into her. The barbs buried deeper into her flesh. He pulled back from her hair and looked into her face. He held the sides of her head and licked the tears from her cheek. Andria looked up and saw his eyes change from brown to an opaque silver. She could see herself in those eyes. She convulsed one more time and then lay still. Andria saw that tears streamed down his face. She reached up and brushed them away. Gan cried. Gan sobbed, "You will give me your pain."

Gan received her pain. He saw what she spoke to him. Gan not only saw Andria. He felt pulled into her memories, then pulled into her body. He saw what she saw. The man who touched her when she was a child. He was pulled into that little girl. He felt that man's touch. He felt her hymen break. He felt the pain of it. He felt the shame. He felt the blood between her legs. Gan shook his head.

This had never happened before. Confessions. He was only meant to gain confessions not be forced into their memories. He could feel her, feel what was done to her. He was displaced, lost. Why did he wipe her makeup away? Why did he bandage her? Was it his kindness that was bringing on this punishment? This feeling of violation? Shame? Disgust? He wanted to dislodge from her, but his body craved her pain. He couldn't pull the barbs back. They were driven deep into her. He was still in her body years later. Snorting cocaine and fucking a client's fiancé. He was in her body as she puked in a toilet, her toilet. He was in her body as she sliced her arm with a razor. He felt the pain. He felt the relief. He sighed as she sighed as she looked at the blood pool on her arms. Now her arms were his arms. Gan shook his head again and looked down at Andria. She was staring into his silver eyes. The barbs pulled out of her. It was just his cock now. It was just his soft brown eyes now.

"I'm so sorry for you," Gan said.

Andria began to laugh. She pulled his face to hers and kissed him. She grabbed his buttocks driving him deeper inside of her. Gan picked her up and swung Andria on her stomach. She grabbed at the mattress as he entered her again. He couldn't look at her. He had to finish this. He had to leave. He wanted it to be quick, but it wasn't. Their sweat drenched the sheets. Andria grabbed her headboard as he thrusted himself repeatedly inside of her. Gan pulled her hands from the headboard and pushed her head to the pillows. Andria tried to turn to face Gan. He forced her head down. He couldn't look at her. "Your pain is mine. Your pain is mine," he kept saying to her. The barbs came out again. They shouldn't have, but they did. They scraped her insides as he thrust himself in and out. He couldn't stop himself. Andria screamed. Gan felt as if he was still in Andria's body. He was now her and him at the same time. Fucking and being fucked. He started to laugh. "Your pain is mine. No! Stop! Stop!" He yelled as he came inside her. Andria was sobbing. Gan pulled out of her, her blood seeping into the sheets. He held her close as she shivered.

Gan should have left, but he didn't. He kissed her tear-soaked cheeks. He placed his hand over her pounding heart. He slid his hand between her legs and felt the gush of their cum mingled with blood. "I'm sorry I hurt you," he said. Gan should have left, but he couldn't. He knew the warning. He knew the signs, but he ignored them. Gan uttered the words he had been warned against ever saying. He pulled Andria close. He nuzzled her neck. "You're so beautiful. So fucking perfect. Never felt this before." Gan swallowed hard. "I love you."

It was sealed. Andria felt Gan's hand at her side. After he spoke the words, "I love you" the pressure of his hands lifted. Andria rolled over slowly. The pain between her thighs exploded. Yet, she turned. She saw no one in her bed. She pulled herself up. She felt the wet sheets. There was evidence of what happened: sweat, blood, and cum. She was alone. Gan was gone.

Andria woke up with a headache that demanded attention. She sat up in bed and looked at her twisted blankets and sheets. Bad dreams? The sheets were damp and cold. There was a foreign scent on her pillows, aftershave and cologne. She swung her legs over the side of the bed and saw clothes piled in the middle of her bedroom floor. A man's t-shirt, a man's pair of jeans, boxer shorts, and socks. Andria rubbed her aching head trying to make sense of her surroundings, of her disheveled bedroom. She looked at her door and saw a pair of navy blue Chucks on the floor. A man was here. A man must still be here. No way he would just walk out naked. She picked up her robe from her chair, put it on, and opened her bedroom door.

Hello? Andria wanted to say that out loud, but she had seen too many horror movies. She grabbed a pair of Ghinger scissors off her dresser. She smirked at the sight of the shears in her hand. She was supposed to be making a quilt. She was supposed to be snipping pieces of fabric, and with each little piece, she should have been sewing back the strengths of her life, what was important to her, what had meaning to her. That's what her support group had suggested. It seemed like a brilliant idea at the time, a way to get her mind off the negative and build something positive, something that could keep her warm at night. Instead of working on her quilt, Andria went out drinking with her friends. Her friends. Andria rubbed her head again. Who was she out with? Did she black out again? Her throbbing head made it difficult to think. Was it Hanna? Beth? Both of them? Neither of them? And whose clothes were in her bedroom?

There was no sign of a man in her hallway. No one in her living room. Dining room was empty. In her kitchen—nothing but a sinkful of dirty dishes. There was only one room left. She opened the bathroom door. Slowly. Nothing there but her fluffy purple towel and more dirty laundry piled in the corner. She had definitely had sex. Her insides ached. She needed to pee. She needed to have an STD test. No reason for a pregnancy test. Her womb had been sucked out of her three years ago. A choice between constant removal of fibroids or a single surgery. She chose the latter.

There was no man here. Andria turned on the shower and took off her robe. It was her day off, and she had so much to do. She had to clean her house. She had groceries to buy. She had a quilt to stitch. She felt the hot water on her flesh. Her crotch and asshole burned as the soap seeped in her crevices. She grasped the walls of the shower. Andria began to cry. She didn't know why she cried. An empty feeling crept in. She looked at her razor. It would be so easy to go back there. Back to the quick release. Just pop the blade and pull the sharpness against her skin. Just to let the pain be felt in reality.

Andria turned off the water, stepped from the shower, and stood naked in front of the mirror. She wiped the moisture from the glass and looked at her naked flesh. She saw her plump breasts in the mirror. Her hands went up and touched her nipples, then travelled from her breasts down her empty womb to her shaven crotch. She wanted to touch it, to touch herself. Instead the tears buckled against her eyelids. She wiped her tears from her face and smeared them against the mirror.

Andria looked into the mirror. It was her face, her sad,

exhausted face. The bags under her eyes were deeper set. *What did I drink last night?* "I want to love you," she whispered to her reflection. She placed her hand on the mirror as if to cradle her face. "I want to. I do, but I can't."

The mirror rippled, then cracked. It cut her. She pulled her fingers to her mouth, and swearing, sucked at the blood. She looked into her own brown eyes. She looked at her long, curly hair. She looked at her tan skin. It all bubbled and rippled. The eyes were only constant. She held her bloody hand up as the mirror vibrated. The brown eyes stayed constant, but the contours changed. She brought her bloody fingers to her mouth and sucked at the blood, trying to cease the bleeding. As she did so, her soft jaw became chiseled. Shoulders widened. Her supple throat rippled and thrust forth an Adam's apple. Muscles imploded over her biceps and triceps. Her breasts shrunk and became enlarged with a masculine mass. Andria screamed, but her reflection stood as stone. A man in her mirror. She started to remember that face, that gentle inviting face from the bar last night.

"You." Andria grabbed her towel.

"Yes, sweetie, me. Don't bother with the towel. Afraid we're past all of that, aren't we?"

"You talk!" Andria dropped her towel on the floor. She grabbed for it, trying to cover herself, then hit her head against the wall. She crumpled to the floor.

"Oh, darling, you are the clumsiest girl I ever did see. No high heels on today. Can't imagine the damage if you had your heels. You girls and your heels, always trying to be cute."

"Shut up." Andria picked herself up from her tiled bathroom floor. "Just stop."

"Stop what? Being stuck here in your mirror? It's my fault, really. Just had to say it. Stupid, stupid, stupid!" He struck his head. Andria's hand lifted at the same time striking her head. She tried to stop, but she had no control over her hand. It kept striking and striking.

"Stop!" Her towel fell again to the floor. She drew closer to the mirror. *Gan.* "Your name is Gan."

"That was curious," he said. "You did what I did. How strange."

"Yes, fabulous." Andria grabbed her towel again, "No, this isn't happening."

"Afraid it is. Trust me—"

"Trust you? What happened last night? What was in that flask?"

"This is odd. Usually I'm not here for that part."

"No, you took advantage. I was. I was," Andria said as she turned at the mirror and lifted her hand, ready to strike.

"Don't go there," Gan said his fist lifted in the mirror. "We both wanted this." Gan pressed his fingers against the glass. Andria's hand lifted and pushed the air around her.

"Please stop moving. You're making me move."

"We both wanted this. Need this. I supplied a service is all. Now, I'm fucked here in your fuck all mirror."

"Just stop talking. You're not real." She turned to the mirror.

"You are not real." Andria started counting. "One, two three, four. One, two, three, four." She took the towel from her body and covered the mirror. She could hear Gan as she left the bathroom.

"I'm the fucking victim here. Put yourself in my place. Where are you going!"

"I have to meet with a client."

"Looking like that? You still have mascara under your eyes. Let me help you."

Andria shut the door and walked naked back to her bedroom. She was still counting, taking in deep breaths, letting the air out from her lungs as her hands shook. "Your counting won't make it all go away. I'll be here when you get back." Gan's muffled voice filled her head.

Andria couldn't concentrate on her meeting. She couldn't get the image of Gan trapped in her mirror out of her head: standing there, naked, their movements in sync with each other. She went through the motions of the meeting, discussing different tablecloths with the bride to be, but her mind wandered back to her sweat-soaked sheets. She went over the champagne flutes with her client. Of course, the right inscriptions would be written on the glass. She looked at the flutes and remembered every orifice Gan entered the night before. Yes? Yes, there would be the perfect lighting for the couple's first dance. Perfect lighting for the honeymoon suite as well, complete with rose petals shaped in a heart on their bed.

During her meeting, Andria didn't see her client's face, that excited bride describing what she wanted for her perfect day. No, instead Andria saw a man trapped in glass in her apartment, his clothes still lying in the middle of her bedroom floor. She tried to go through the motions. At one point, she felt herself looking off past her client, dazed. She even felt her jaw drop a bit. She ceased breathing through her nose, and just breathed through her mouth as if she were still trapped in the sweaty sheets from last night. She could still feel every orifice filled by him, the thing called Gan.

She came back to reality. "Yes," she said. "We always have champagne flutes for the wedding party. Would you like them engraved? If so I need you to fill this out." She handed a form to her client. Name of the client? Who cared. Andria didn't, not at that point. This prima donna bride to be. Andria was being too hard on her. Not this bitch's fault that she was happy, and that Andria was— well what was Andria exactly? Her client just looked at her and offered a fake smile.

"You came highly recommended. I'm sure it will be wonderful."

"Yes, it will be your perfect day." Andria saw her out, shut the door, and slid to the floor. She tried to keep the tears from falling. It was as if something had opened in her. She hadn't felt this exposed in years, not since she was in therapy. She needed to pull herself together. She had another client in an hour. The empty statements filled her head. *Yes, we will have the perfect lighting. Yes, we will decorate your suite with rose petals. Yes, of course we have champagne flutes. You want doves?* Cliché. *We can get doves. Yes, I will go back to my empty house. I will see his clothes still on my floor. I have lost my mind. I will see him in the mirror as my reflection.*

Andria crawled back to her desk and lifted herself into the chair. She had to meet this next client, but all she wanted was sleep. She opened her compact to check the puffiness in her eyes— and looked in the mirror. There he was. Again. Andria screamed.

"Hello, dearie. I've missed you."

Andria's hands trembled. "This isn't happening." Andria stood up, gawking at the open compact on her desk. Gan just grinned.

"What's not happening?" he asked. "Oh, don't look at us like that. If anything, I should be the one upset. At least you get to walk around and live your life. I'm the one stuck in here."

Andria glared at the mirror. "Do you ever shut up?"

"Oh, your makeup. Have you been crying?"

Andria sat down and shut the compact. She held her head in her hands. The compact began to bounce around her desk knocking itself into her laptop. She could hear his muffled voice. "Still here, sweetie."

Andria glared at the compact and sighed.

"Still here. Come on. Open me up. It's been boring in here. Would've said something earlier, but seemed you were busy."

Andria picked up the compact and opened it. There was his face looking back at her. She started to cry again. "That's it. I'm losing my mind. Time to just call me doctor and go back."

"No, no. No," Gan said. "You're not losing your mind. This is all my fault really."

"I'm not disagreeing."

"But it is. I couldn't help myself. You're not like the other girls. Usually they are, how to put this delicately"—Gan looked off then turned his eyes back to Andria—"they were more innocent."

"Innocent?"

"Well, maybe that's the wrong term. Not as damaged. I picked the wrong bird was all. Had no idea all you had been through, the pain, and then the sex. I did feel it coming from you. Should've known better, but it was so intoxicating. That smell. That pain. I fell for it, and now I'm here."

"That simple."

"That simple."

Andria picked up her cell phone.

"What are you doing?" Gan asked.

"Calling my doctor."

"Andria hang up. Please. I don't want to go there," Gan pleaded, but Andria continued scrolling through her contacts. "You have a meeting. We can make this work."

Andria looked at him.

"Just trust me. Hang up the phone and take out your makeup."

Andria looked at Gan in her compact. She wiped a tear from her eye. As her hand moved, so did his, wiping away an invisible tear. "Ok." She dug into her purse and placed her makeup on the desk.

"Concealer first," Gan said. "Just look at me and don't fight me."

Andria lifted the concealer.

"I move you move. You move I move. We have at least established that." Gan lifted his hand to his under eye and blotted. Andria's hand moved, and she felt the concealer being applied to her skin.

Andria wasn't hungry when she got home. She wanted sleep. She wanted her heels off. She wanted to be naked under her purple sheets. She wanted her thoughts to stop lecturing her. Her client had loved her makeup. Andria admitted that she didn't do her own makeup today. The blushing bride begged to know who he was. Could she hire him? How could Andria tell her client that the makeup artist was her own deranged delusion, or better yet a one-night stand with some demonic force that was now trapped in her mirror. *I'm so sorry. He is actually doing a wedding in Nepal on the same date. I'm so sorry.* Andria looked around her apartment. She decided to clean.

Andria cleaned her dishes, dried them, and put them away. Glasses against glasses. Coffee cups lined up with the handles facing to the left. She wiped down her stove and countertops. She swept and mopped the floors. She avoided the mirrors. Andria hadn't realized how many mirrors she owned. She took out the laundry and hung towels over the mirrors, hung towels over his face. She had her ear buds in blasting Purity Ring just so she wouldn't have to hear his voice begging her to look at him. Andria opened a bottle of wine and poured herself a glass. She sat in her living room, but she was facing a floor-length mirror. The towel moved as if breathing.

She stood up with her glass still in her left hand. She touched the fabric of the towel and felt a hot breath. She pulled down the towel. He stood in front of her in the full-length mirror, fully naked. He didn't mimic her movements this time. His hand reached through the mirror and grabbed her wrist. Gan stepped through the glass.

Her glass of wine crashed, sending wine and glass shards spewing over the hardwood floor she had just cleaned. Andria tried to flee. His grip on her wrist tightened. She tried to shake him off, but he pulled her close to his nakedness.

"It's not too late then," Gan said holding her. Andria began to scream out for help. Gan placed his hand over her mouth as they fell to the floor. Andria punched him and kicked him. Gan grappled Andria and held her by the throat. He placed his hand over her mouth. "You need to shut it now. Hear me?" He looked down at her. Andria shook her head yes. Gan removed his hand. "Clothes. Where are my clothes?"

"They're on the chair in my bedroom."

Gan released her and turned towards the bedroom. "Place looks nice," he said over his shoulder.

Andria looked at the broken glass around her and started swearing. She felt the need to clean it up, but she found it impossible to remove herself from the floor to get her broom and dustpan. Instead she just stared at the glass and listened to Gan fumbling with his clothes. She heard him put on his shirt, zip up his jeans, buckle his belt. "Oh, my watch. It's still here." Gan walked into the living room, admiring his watch. "I always wanted to be a savior type. Not quite in the cards, is it?" He turned to Andria still looking at his watch. "I know it's childish, a grown man having a Superman watch, but I admire your heroes." He looked up at the mirror and shivered. "Fucking cold in there." He walked towards Andria then stopped short. "I need to go. I'd hug you or kiss you, but I don't know what that would do."

"Please just leave," Andria said, still staring at the broken glass.

Gan hesitated for a moment. He watched Andria as if trying to decide something Andria as she stared at the smashed wine glass. "Alright, I'm off."

Andria didn't answer. Gan walked to the front door and tried to turn the door knob. It wouldn't turn. He pulled on the door, but it wouldn't budge. "What in the holy fuck," he grunted. Andria looked over her shoulder at him. Gan pulled at the door. He kicked it. It wouldn't budge. "Is there some sort of secret lock you have on this fucking door?"

Andria didn't want this man in her house anymore. She could tell by looking at the lock that the door was unlocked. "A little help!" She heard him yelling at her. She pushed herself from the floor and walked to the door.

"It's unlocked," she said as she opened the door. Gan attempted to walk through it. The door swung shut. They both stood there stunned. Andria turned to Gan. Tears streamed down her cheeks. "Leave. Leave. Leave!" She pushed Gan's chest throwing him into the wall. "I want you to get out!"

"I can't!"

Andria punched Gan in the mouth. He lifted his hand to his lips and felt the loose tooth. He felt the blood gush between his fingers. He tried to move away from her fists, but he was pinned against the wall. He tried to keep her away from his blood, but she was coming at him too fast.

Some of his blood fell from his mouth and landed in her eye. That's when her assault on Gan stopped. Andria fell to her knees holding her face. The mirror moaned as if to crack, as if it was pushing against the wooden frame. Gan kneeled down next to her. "Let me see," he said trying to take a hold of her face.

Andria pushed his hand away from her. "Get away from me," she said as she rocked back and forth on the floor.

"Andria, look at me," Gan said as he sat next to her. "I need to see your eyes."

Andria uncovered her face. She still had her eyes shut. A mixture of tears and blood ran down her face.

"You have to open your eyes. Please."

Andria opened her eyes. Her once brown irises were speckled with silver. The silver moved like mercury until it turned her irises completely silver.

"Can you see?"

"Yes, but it's different now." Andria started to cry. "Everything is so bright. And you, I see this color around you. A dark blue color all around you." Andria sobbed. "I can see it, that sadness. Make it go away."

Gan brushed her tears away. "Afraid I can't do that." He looked at the door. How close he was from leaving. "Fuck all," he said.

Andria unbuttoned her shirt. Gan sat still, holding his head in his hand. She reached out for him. He felt the energy from her fingertips. He remembered his childhood. He let Andria kiss him. His heart ached as he felt his father's fists against his head, a feeling he had forgotten for over twenty years. He uttered the words his father screamed at him. *Embarrassment. Useless. Stupid.*

"Let it out," Andria said as she unzipped his pants. "Tell me your pain," she said as she put him inside of her. Gan's thoughts branched from his father to the women he had lain with, the women he drove to madness, the women he had collected confessions from, the women who then later took their lives.

"I can't," he cried as she rode him faster.

She held his neck to the floor.

"You can. You will." Andria leaned over and licked the blood from his lips. "You will give me all of your pain."

Gan heard the mirror finally crack. He felt his lips move. He knew that he was talking. He felt a sense of shame as he looked in Andria's silver eyes.

SHIKSA

Rachel wonders why Jacob is screaming. Just a moment ago he kissed her and now he's screaming, his hands trembling, tears crawling closer to his clammy cheeks. She watches as he digs his fingers through his hair, as if he could pull the blond locks out by their roots. She yells as Jacob stumbles out her front door, but he doesn't acknowledge her, doesn't look back. The front door slams. Did the house shake?

Rachel runs towards the front door, but she feels a pull in her belly. It is then that she sees the object of his distress. It is her. Rachel looks in the bathtub and sees her lifeless body bobbing in bloody water. Her arms are cut as the blood seeps over the edge of the tub. There is an empty bottle of scotch next to the tub and a bottle of her Xanax opened. Only two pills remain on the bath mat of the thirty. The house shakes again. Or is she shaking? It is then that Rachel realizes that it can't be her shaking. She feels nothing.

* * *

Every night she comes. There is no shaking of tree branches scratching at the windows, no creaking of the floor boards. The house does not shift. There is no cold air, no dark shadows against the wall. Everything he has ever seen or heard of a haunting is a fucking lie. What there is: heaviness of air—so thick he feels his skin lift away from the meat of his flesh. This thickness permeates his lungs with the scent of her. Lavender and mint. She loved to grow those herbs in her garden. Now he was the fertilizer for her plantings. Her spade dug into his thighs carving the trenches for the seeds she kept for him. One by one they dropped. Starting at his Adam's apple, a trail laid down his chest, a seed left in his belly button, seeds falling on his groin until he felt her cold flesh around him. Ears echoing moans into drums of a foreign tongue forbidden. He sees a red light illuminate his stomach. He wants to panic, but feels stuck to the bed, unable to lift his arms from his side. The light becomes more vibrant, then forms small orbs of red light. They flow from him and into her. Was it his chi, that root chakra he's heard about? All he knows is the more those orbs form, the more they flow from his and disappear into Rachel, the more turned on he becomes. He licks at the empty air. A baby cries. He clamps his eyelids, trying to bury them under the shallow skull frame of his face. Leah moans and reaches over. Hard again. Shit.

"Jacob? Really?"

"Sorry." Jacob thinks of his grandmother, the gangrene he saw on his patient's foot, but his cock is stubborn, Rachel's recently conquered flag pole. "I can—

"No, I got him." Leah leaves Jacob to his hard on to tend to their crying baby. Eyes, red and angry, appear above his. Jacob tries to swallow. He feels her thickness. The hands gathered at his throat. He can't hear her as her mouth moves over him. He feels her. *You left me there. You left me.* Every night for the past week it has been the same. Thickness, floating, apple seeds, whispering, fucking. Uncomfortable hard on. A wife he should love. A lover he left in blood.

Rachel always stares into Jacob. She would never leave his side, even though he had left her there to die, bleeding out in her tub. She is and always would be there. She had to breathe on him her heavy "fuck you" death breath. *I am here, Jacob. I am here*—death breath—*Touch it, Jacob. Touch US.* Every time, Leah would leave the bed. And every time Jacob would lie there with his hard on. Rachel waits again. Jacob sighs. Rachel slides in him. Jacob cries. *Sing me your Songs of Solomon.*

"No." Jacob tugs at the sheet.

Solomon.

"No." Panting. Sweating. Erection. Rachel smiles. Cock tilted. Her mouth opens. Spill. Release. Swallow. Sobs. Kisses follow. Kisses always follow.

Thank you, Jacob. Licking and kisses follow. *Jacob, don't drink.*

"What?"

Shh. The baby.

Jacob feels Rachel pull away. The sheets billow for a moment over his body, then slowly fall into a cocoon around his clammy skin.

Jacob calls into work. He stays upstairs, away from Leah and his son, Isaac. Leah brings him tomato soup. Leah makes him mint tea. Jacob wants her to go away. Leave him to his vaporous lover. Isaac cries and Leah scurries away. Once again, Rachel appears. Why didn't he stay? Why didn't he call the cops? Because he's married to Leah, a good, wholesome Jewess. How could he explain Rachel, his Shiksa? He should have never answered her email asking him to reconnect, but it had been over twenty years since Jacob last saw her. How was she? Was she successful? What career path did she choose? Did she have kids? Ever get married? Did she gain weight? Was she still hot? Those questions and Jacob's parents drew him back to Ithaca. He should have stayed in Maine, but he went, egged on by Leah and his parents: go back home, check out the position, your parents need you. *Jacob needs Rachel.*

Jacob hadn't met Rachel in public. She didn't want people to talk. He memorized her address from her email. A small house on the outskirts of the Commons. Her new home. Her new beginning. His return.

Jacob remembers seeing her again. Her hair still dark brown, only a couple of hairs turned grey with age. There is a small crease from laugh lines. Rachel is thicker than he remembered, but they are both in their forties. It's to be expected. Her breasts are full and high. Rachel says to Jacob, "I strapped them down when I was pregnant. I'm too vain for saggy tits. You like them?"

You like them? No. That wasn't what she said all those years ago when they were just seventeen. She transferred to his school in her senior year. He had never been around a girl like Rachel. *Jacob, do you like these? They like you.* So fucking cheesy, but her bra wasn't: white lace with underwire. She lifted her shirt as they left the diner. She laughed at him again. She knew he couldn't have her. But she showed him anyway. *Here they are. Like them?* That giggle. Those dimples in her cheeks. That laugh. At him. His parents didn't help. Jacob thought they wanted him to be tortured by her. They knew full well she wasn't Jewish. They knew the way he looked at her. Yet, Jacob's parents insisted that Rachel always be at his side. Invite Rachel to Sabbath. Invite Rachel to Passover. Invite Rachel to you brother's Bar Mitzvah. And what did Rachel do? Twirl in her beautiful polka dot dress until it lifted. Jacob ran onto the dance floor, but it was too late. Simon, his little brother, saw everything on the pink, silk fury of her Victoria's Secret underwear.

"Rachel, seriously!"

"Oh." She laughed, kissing his ear, pretending to whisper. Rachel pulled back. "He's becoming a man!" He scorned Rachel for what she showed, what he wanted kept a secret. He never saw her upper thighs until that night. He never saw her pink underwear until she twirled for his thirteen-year-old brother. Her dimples mocked him. Blue and white polka dot dress and pink panties chuckled, "You cannot touch this." Ha. Ha. Ha. Fuck her. He had to fuck her.

They went for walks. She lived around the block, and now he wonders how he was always at her house. Homework or something and another. Jacob thought he was so smart. She was just a girl in his high school, and truth be told, they never had a single class together. So why was Rachel invited to all of HIS holidays? Rachel, what did she believe in anyway? *I'm a truth seeker.* That's what she always said. What did that even mean?

"What the hell does it mean?"

"Sweetie, you're burning up." Leah wipes Jacob's forehead. "I'll get you some water."

Jacob tries to push himself up in the bed. He feels faint and falls back to the pillows. "No," he says. "I'm fine."

"I'm giving you one more day. Then you have to go to the doctor.

"Yes, one more day." Jacob watches Leah leave. She takes the trash can with her that he vomited in. He smells lavender and mint. Rachel. The sheets rise again. Rachel descends. He feels her on his skin. Her lips are on his ears moving gently at the lobes. He closes his eyes as the seeds trickle against his skin. Apples. There are always apple seeds.

Open your eyes. Jacob doesn't want to. It's just another trick of his mind, another delusion. Rachel is dead. Rachel is gone. Rachel kisses him. Rachel presses her breasts against his sweaty t-shirt. *Open your eyes.* His eye lids feel stuck, but they do open, slowly, aching against the dryness. Rachel looks at him, dimples. Those dimples. Her brown hair falls against his damp shirt. She places her finger on his lips as she gyrates on him. She's not so cold now. She feels like tepid water as her hips rotate. *Shh. The baby is awake.*

Of course, Isaac is awake. What does she want? Jacob tries to look away, but Rachel has a hold of his chin with her lukewarm fingers. She leans over and kisses him. Jacob tries not to moan. His thoughts drift to the past, to his parents' wood panel station wagon...

There was a large sign that said, "Thomas White for Mayor." It was May. Jacob would be going off to the University of Rochester for college; Rachel wanted to take a year off to reflect. In both of their minds it was now or never. Rachel was underneath him. Legs spread. Top open, white lace bra inviting. She laughed at him when they first started kissing. He grabbed her face and kissed her neck, her face, those cheeks with the dimples. And she laughed. "Your kisses sound like Qbert jumping off blocks." She just laughed. He went for her breasts and shoved her bra up. "Ow!" She smacked him. "It's an underwire!" Too late. He was inside her. The slapping turned to grabbing. Her hands dug into his back. He drove deeper, his lips pressed against the lace of her bra. The underwire snapped, and he tasted blood as the metal bit into the skin of his lips.

She reached up to his face as she tried to sit up. Jacob saw headlights in the parking lot. He pushed Rachel back against the seat. "Shit!"

"What?"

"Nothing. Stay down." Jacob kept thrusting as he held Rachel closer to the seat. She put her hands on his chest. She could feel his heart pounding. Jacob plunged deeper. Rachel closed around him. Jacob bit her earlobe. He moaned. He groaned. His nails tore at the flesh of her outer thighs. Rachel's teeth grazed Jacob's skin, her hot breath on his Adam's apple.

"Uh, where are we?" Rachel moaned. She pushed against Jacob, attempting to get up.

"Shh, just keep your head down." He drove in deeper. Rachel arched her back. Fluid flowed around him. Jacob cried, diving deeper.

"Where are we?" she asked again.

"My temple."

"Fuck...you...Jacob."

He didn't mind her cursing him. He could care less if his god cursed him for crossing into the gentile divide. Her nails scratched his back as her virginal blood crept past his cock. She looked as if she was going to cry.

"You okay?" Jacob asked.

"Yes, just kiss me."

Jacob kissed her, feeling her breath enter his lungs and tears sting his clammy cheeks. He couldn't say that he felt complete or whole. He thought he would feel that way during his first time, that moment of oneness with another person. He felt split apart—his desperate, animalistic need overpowering the dutiful son—holding his friend in a greedy embrace, determined to devour every inch of her taboo flesh. *Fuck me.* Thrust. *You at Seder.* Thrust. *You and that low-cut shirt teasing my cantor.* Thrust. *You and that blue—*

thrust—*and white*—thrust—*polka dot dress*. Thrust. Thrust. Thrust. Jacob could feel Rachel's tears on his chest. He looked down at her.

"I love you, Jacob." She looked into his eyes for a moment then looked away. Jacob grabbed her face and turned her gaze back at him. "I'm sorry. I do."

"What?" Thrust.

"I love you." Rachel tried to look away again, but Jacob wouldn't let her. "Just kiss me. Just kiss me," she panted in his ear. *Just keep kissing me.*

Today, it is different. He feels more than the covers hovering over his hard on. He feels moisture. He feels a swelling. He feels velvet. He feels himself flow into Rachel as she had flowed around him over twenty years ago. Fuck... You...

SHIKSA. She whispers that word in his ear. It must be her. Must be Rachel. He opens his eyes and dares to look up. Rachel. She is laughing as she rides him into the mattress. *The baby's awake.* She laughs again. Jacob reaches up and touches her arms still bleeding everywhere on the sheets, on his bare flesh. *Put your head down. Just keep your head down.*

For forty days and forty nights this seduction continues. Jacob weaker. Rachel stronger. White hair grips hold of his roots, at first speckled, then filling in at the sides of his head. His mind drifts off to the back of his parents' station wagon and the email Rachel sent him three months ago. Why did he do it? Why did he come back? He had to see her. His life played out for him just as he'd planned: a great job at the hospital, a loving Jewish wife, beautiful house, beautiful son. What did Rachel gain over the years? Rachel gave him the answer over the first night they reunited in her house. The scotch flowed, and Rachel told all. Her mother and brother had passed. A sudden miscarriage launched her into a divorce. She had lovers off and on, but her life had been a lonely one. The scotched poured, and soon Jacob's tongue wagged. He wished he had travelled more. He wished he had dated more. He wished he had seen and experienced more. He wished he had been there more for her.

The scotch didn't only loosen their tongues. Before long, Jacob and Rachel were naked and in her bed, reliving high school passions with their middle-aged bodies. The clumsy love-making of their youth had been perfected over the years. There was no more shyness, no more fumbling, just earnest and devoted exploration of the flesh that had been denied them for so many years.

That night of rekindled exploration turned into an affair. Perhaps it was too hard on Rachel. Jacob couldn't leave his wife. What would his community think? His colleagues? His parents? Was that why she decided to end it all? Once again, Jacob felt he had let Rachel down. Once again, he wasn't there for her. Yet, Rachel didn't go down peacefully. That was never her style. She lingers in his room every night waiting for his son to stir, forcing Leah to leave, so she can rape Jacob all over again. Stronger Rachel. Weaker Jacob. He should end this once and for all. His concentration is fractured at best and his lectures lately have been scattered. Colleagues are noticing, and the new fellows start their positions today. Jacob needs to get his shit together.

Jacob hears Rachel's words still as he readies himself for the day. *The baby is awake.* No shit, you woke him. *Don't drink. Don't drink.* Rachel repeats those words as she rides on top of him, kissing and licking his ears. Don't drink what? But Rachel only smiles, and as Leah opens the door, Rachel disappears again.

* * *

Isaac is now sleeping through the night. Leah no longer leaves his side, and Jacob is left to sleep soundly. Rachel no longer haunts him. Although Jacob feels relief at Rachel's disappearance, he still feels a pang of abandonment and loss. Perhaps the whole event was in his head. Perhaps it was his sick way of grieving.

Work returns to normal. He is focused and turns the passion he had for Rachel towards the department. The fellowship had begun to fall apart during his encounters, imagined or not, with his dead lover. The fellows were slacking: not studying, not attending conferences. He needs to whip them into shape. One fellow stands out, Lilian Davies. She's bright. She's eager, but seems to be cracking under pressure. The nurses find her to be rude, and there are complaints from the staff and patients as well.

Jacob finishes up his office notes, preparing to meet Lilian and go over her progress. There's a meek knock on his office door. At least she's prompt. Jacob signs off his computer and walks to the door. He opens the door, and Dr. Davies is standing in front of him, her eyes looking to the floor.

"Lilian, have a seat."

Lilian sits down as Jacob goes back to his desk.

"We need to discuss your progress."

"I understand."

"When you first started here in July, you were spot on. Your cases for the Friday Morning Conference were interesting and insightful. The patients and staff thought you were courteous and professional, but lately there have been several complaints, and you failed your ESAP-ITE exam. I understand that it's the holiday season, and things can be quite hectic."

"I don't celebrate the holidays," Lilian said. "I'm not religious and really don't have a family."

"Okay, so what's going on?"

"I actually picked this university to be closer to my aunt, but unfortunately we never connected. She was the last living person from my family, but she passed away before I could find her. I was hoping that you could tell me about her."

"Uhm, do I know her?"

"Very well. Her name was Rachel. Rachel Haggerty. I've been researching her, and apparently you both went to high school together."

Jacob shifts in his chair. His hands start to sweat. "Rachel is—I mean was—your aunt?"

"Yes, I'm her brother's daughter. When my parents died in a car accident, I went to live with my grandmother on my mother's side. She passed away two years ago. I wanted to track down Rachel, maybe learn more about my family."

"I'm so sorry about the loss of your family." Jacob takes a sip of his coffee. Coffee. He shouldn't be drinking coffee right now; his heart is pounding, his palms sweating, his throat feels like it is swelling, his leg is shaking, the nerve in his temple is throbbing. Rachel. Now something else is throbbing. "It was so tragic what happened to Rachel."

"It just seems that everyone in my life dies. Christ, I'm sorry. I shouldn't have brought this up. It's been so long since you knew my aunt."

Jacob looks at her, and he sees Rachel—the brown hair and the hazel green eyes, the dimples in her cheeks, the vein that throbs in her forehead the same way it did with Rachel when she was upset. Something isn't sitting right with Jacob. He looks at Lilian again. "I don't mean to pry, but your last name is Davies. Why isn't it Haggerty?"

"My parents never married. They were actually just getting back together when they got in the accident. I have my mother's last name."

"I'm sorry. It wasn't my business."

"No, it's okay. Do you have a tissue?"

"Yes, sorry." Jacob grabbed his box of tissues and placed it in front of her. He felt badly for her, watching Lilian fall apart. "I do know some things from when we were in high school, and I did know your father for a time." Maybe this is his chance to make everything right.

"I apologize for letting my personal life interfere with my professionalism. It has been eating me up inside for quite some time now."

"No, Lilian, it's fine. I want to be here for you. And yes, I can tell you about your family. To be honest, I have struggled with the passing of your aunt. It would be a comfort for me to share what I know."

"Thank you, but maybe this isn't the right place. I really don't want my colleagues knowing about this. I'm sorry to put this on you, but I really would like some closure. Are you busy this evening?"

"No, I'm free." But he wasn't free. Jacob would never be free. He should have said no. He should have kept the conversation professional. He should not have acknowledged that he knew this woman's family. He shouldn't have fucked her aunt. He should just go home to his wife, but Jacob was not free. He was ensnared once again.

Jacob meets Lilian at Penelope's Bistro. It has a quaint, café-like atmosphere. There is a woman sitting on a bar stool playing classical guitar—"Asturias" by Isaac Albéniz. Jacob is not sure if he should be entranced by the fast plucking or take it as a foreboding message to get up and leave. He loosens his ties and sits at the table to wait.

At the hospital, Lilian is fierce, but here in this small restaurant she is demure. She is wearing a light blue dress with little silver flowers inlaid at the neckline, not the usual black or navy-blue pant suit Jacob is accustomed to seeing her in. The special is braised pork tenderloin. They both decline and order the baked chicken. A glass of chardonnay turns into a bottle. Jacob tells Lilian the story of how her aunt pretended to be sick in high school because she was late to class.

"Why was she late?"

"She was flirting with, with, oh what was his name?" Jacob pours the last of the wine in his glass. "Michael. Michael Brent!" He slapped the table and laughs. "Turns out he was gay, but neither of them knew it at the time."

"Really." Lilian flags down the waitress. "Can we get another bottle?"

"No, coffee," Jacob says.

"Two cappuccinos." Lilian turns back to Jacob. "So, why did she have to pretend that she was sick?"

"Well, her teacher wouldn't let her in the class without a pass. Rachel never missed a class. She saw me in the hall and was freaking out. Then she got this brilliant idea to pretend that her sugar dropped. Her mother, your grandmother, was a diabetic, so Rachel knew the symptoms." Jacob runs his fingers through his greying hair. "I was studying to be an EMT, so I acted like I found her in the hallway all woozy. I escorted her to the nurse, and we tried not to giggle behind the curtains as I acted like the concerned classmate."

"Wow, the two of you. What a pair."

Jacob sets his wine glass down. He looks at Lilian. She has

Rachel's eyes, so unnerving the way she looks through him. "Will you excuse me? I need to make a phone call."

"Of course." Lilian smiles. Dimples.

Jacob doesn't make a phone call. Jacob looks into the mirror of the men's bathroom. "What are you doing?" He turns on the faucet and splashes the frigid water on his face. He dries off his face and looks in the mirror. "Drink your damn coffee and go the fuck home to your wife. Rachel is dead."

* * *

The floor is cold. The floor is hard. Jacob tries to move, but he feels lethargic. His eyes feel plastered shut. He is the statue of David lying on a cold marble tiled floor. There is a flutter above him, and he sees without looking: blue fabric with silver flowers. He forces his eyes open. Lilian holds him by the throat as she rides him into the marble floor. Lilian. No. What has he done? He tries to move, but his arms are dead weight. She holds his neck to the floor and laughs.

"Lilian, stop. Stop." Jacob tries to look around, but his head is pounding. "Where am I?"

Lilian bends over. She bites his ear so hard that she rips the skin. Jacob screams. "Don't recognize it?" Lilian asks. "It's your temple." Lilian sits upright and her face shifts. A red ball glows above her head. It descends and falls over Lilian's face, but Lilian doesn't seem to notice. Jacob smells lavender. Jacob smells mint. Jacob hears Rachel. *I said don't drink. The baby is awake.* Instead of Lilian, Jacob now sees Rachel. *Put your head down.*

"I don't understand!" Jacob tries to push Lilian off him.

"Oh, he doesn't understand. You and your great fucking life. You shallow pig. You don't understand."

"Get off me. What the fuck did you do? Get off!"

"Working on it, daddy." Lilian reaches into her purse and pulls out a knife. "Almost there."

The glowing red ball flitters above him and descends into his abdomen. "Get off me!" Jacob shouts, shoving Lilian so hard that he sends her crashing into the wall. And Rachel won't stop speaking to him. *The baby is awake. The baby is awake.* Jacob gets to his knees and pulls up his pants. He staggers across the floor. Lilian screams as she searches for her knife. *Jacob, run!*

"I can't. I can't." Jacob's knees weaken and he falls to the floor. He pulls his weight across the floor and tries to hide behind a pew.

"Oh, Jacob David Tattelbaum. Years ago, you fucked my mom. Found her diaries, and now she's dead. You will wish I'd never lived. Lilian staggers around with her knife. Lilian, the temple, Rachel not speaking to him anymore. "She gave me up, Jacob. She gave me away. Your shiksa, your whore, my mother. Look at me now, daddy."

Lilian's feet are close. Jacob wants to move, but he can't. "Peek-a-boo. Now I've got you." Lilian kicks him in the chest. Jacob can do nothing but lie there and take his new-found daughter's abuse.

"I didn't know."

"You didn't want to know." Lilian straddles him again. "One

more time, like mom?" She opens his fly and pulls out his penis. "After we're done, I'll slice you open just like your shiksa. Then when you're dead, you can laugh together forever. What a pair. What a pair."

Jacob throws up. Unable to move his head, his vomit sprays out on his daughter's dress and splatters back in his face, burning his eyes. The glowing red light is there again, the light so like the illumination that appeared when Rachel haunted him. The light appears behind Lilian and is growing larger, beginning to take shape and form. Lilian slices open Jacob's left arm. The shape begins to vibrate. Lilian lifts the knife and slices Jacob's right arm. Instead of pain, Jacob feels nothing. When Jacob looks up, he sees Lilian is still with blood pouring from her lips. There is a fist jutting through her chest. The hand holds a beating heart. Lilian collapses and falls to the side. All that is left in front of him is Rachel.

"The baby sleeps. She finally sleeps." Rachel holds her bloody hands to her face. "I'm sorry that I came to you like I did, but I needed your strength."

"I can see you. Really see you." Jacob feels life again. Jacob can move again. He sits up. He reaches for Rachel. "Why didn't you tell me? Why didn't you?"

"Go home, Jacob," Rachel says. "Go home."

ABOUT THE AUTHOR

Lisah Jayne Walden resides in upstate New York with her two children and three cats. She received a double BA in History and English from the University of Rochester and an MA in English from the College at Brockport. Her hobbies include reading and writing horror, watching movies with her kids, and gardening.

FIND LISAH ON SOCIAL MEDIA

https://facebook.com/lisahwalden73
https://twitter.com/LisahZoe974
https://instagram.com/stillwritinglwalden

ACKNOWLEDGMENTS

Many thanks to those who brought me here~

My children, Andrew and Simone, who dealt with a very tired mommy, at times a grumpy mommy. You believed in me and loved me even when I ran out of coffee!

My dad, William, who has always been proud of me. You have watched me transform my life and go back to what I love.

My mother, Nancy. I weep that you are not alive for this moment. You taught me to be a strong, independent woman and to always go for my dreams. I just wish you were alive for this moment. I wish I could feel your kiss on my cheek and your arms around me.

Stephanie Stockmeister. STEF! YOU FUCKING ROCK! We connected at Brockport. You were in my smoky room as I wrote many of these tales. You gave your input, and you provided the beautiful artwork for my book! You were my graduate school comrade.

Fun Barb, I never knew that having a cigarette with you outside of Strong hospital would grant such a strong friendship. You accept my temperament and my mood swings. You showed up to the reading of "The Tea Party" with your Raggedy Ann Doll!!! You always commit to the theme!

Amalia, how can I not thank you... You were the one who opened my eyes as a teenager. I was secluded from the mainstream world. You showed me art and Madonna when my mother wasn't looking. To be friends with you so many years later is incredible.

Elise, yup we butt heads, but hey, girl, we are stubborn as hell. Through and through, with everything, you have been nothing but supportive of me. I remember watching Dorian Gray repeatedly for a paper. You wanted to pull your hair out but stayed with me as I wrote that horrid paper. You also read my short stories. You hosted my first reading. I remember you smiling as I nervously read my story. Horror creeps you out, yet you smiled.

My instructors~ First, Toni Vinci. I learned so much with you. I found my writing soul again. As a child, I was told that a woman should not be a writer. I decided to break free from the Baptist dogma ingrained in me. I saw your passion. You showed your weaknesses and frailty. You made that all acceptable. I was awed by it, the rawness. I wanted that fervor. Next, Joanna Scott, when I wanted to quit your class, you jumped up and hit me on the head with your stack of papers. I needed that! I also want to thank Sarah Higley, who pushed me with my creative thesis; some of those tales are in this collection. I thank James Whorton, JR. who accepted me breaking the rules with my story "The Tea Party." Thank you, Steve Fellner, for stating that I'm not shocking you. I was still dealing with my upbringing. Life is messy. Sex is messy. Messy is not necessarily bad. Ralph Black, I'm not a fan of poetry. After your classes, I learned that every word counts. Your instruction assisted me in flash fiction. Ann Panning, I appreciate the works you had our class read and the focus on humanity.

Lastly, I thank Sara Grace Liu from Three Fates Editing. This has been a long journey. You challenged me in many ways. It has been a grueling adventure. I also thank Courtney Cannon from Fiction Atlas Press. You have been more than patient with me. I found it easier to write than to commit to publishing. You did a wonderful job.